MW01088710

Forever

The Queen's Alpha Series, Volume 5

W.J. May

Published by Dark Shadow Publishing, 2018.

FOREVER

First edition. April 15, 2018.

Written by W.J. May.

Also by W.J. May

Bit-Lit Series
Lost Vampire
Cost of Blood
Price of Death

Blood Red Series
Courage Runs Red
The Night Watch
Marked by Courage
Forever Night

Daughters of Darkness: Victoria's Journey
Victoria
Huntress
Coveted (A Vampire & Paranormal Romance)
Twisted

Hidden Secrets Saga

Seventh Mark - Part 1
Seventh Mark - Part 2
Marked By Destiny
Compelled
Fate's Intervention
Chosen Three
The Hidden Secrets Saga: The Complete Series

Paranormal Huntress Series
Never Look Back
Coven Master
Alpha's Permission

Prophecy Series
Only the Beginning
White Winter
Secrets of Destiny

The Chronicles of Kerrigan
Rae of Hope
Dark Nebula
House of Cards
Royal Tea
Under Fire
End in Sight
Hidden Darkness
Twisted Together
Mark of Fate

Strength & Power
Last One Standing
Rae of Light
The Chronicles of Kerrigan Box Set Books # 1 - 6

The Chronicles of Kerrigan: Gabriel
Living in the Past
Staring at the Future
Present For Today

The Chronicles of Kerrigan Prequel
Question the Darkness
Into the Darkness
Fight the Darkness
Alone in the Darkness
Lost in Darkness
Christmas Before the Magic
The Chronicles of Kerrigan Prequel Series Books #1-3

The Chronicles of Kerrigan Sequel
A Matter of Time
Time Piece
Second Chance
Glitch in Time
Our Time
Precious Time

The Hidden Secrets Saga
Seventh Mark (part 1 & 2)

The Queen's Alpha Series
Eternal
Everlasting
Unceasing
Evermore
Forever
Boundless

The Senseless Series
Radium Halos
Radium Halos - Part 2
Nonsense

Standalone
Shadow of Doubt (Part 1 & 2)
Five Shades of Fantasy
Shadow of Doubt - Part 1
Shadow of Doubt - Part 2
Four and a Half Shades of Fantasy
Dream Fighter
What Creeps in the Night
Forest of the Forbidden
Arcane Forest: A Fantasy Anthology

THE QUEEN'S ALPHA SERIES

FOREVER

USA TODAY BESTSELLING AUTHOR
W . J .   M A Y

Copyright 2018 by W.J. May

THE QUEEN'S ALPHA SERIES

FOREVER

USA TODAY BESTSELLING AUTHOR

W.J. MAY

Have You Read the C.o.K Series?

The Chronicles of Kerrigan

Book I - *Rae of Hope* is FREE!

BOOK TRAILER:

http://www.youtube.com/watch?v=gILAwXxx8MU

How hard do you have to shake the family tree to find the truth about the past?

Fifteen year-old Rae Kerrigan never really knew her family's history. Her mother and father died when she was young and it is only when she accepts a scholarship to the prestigious Guilder Boarding School in England that a mysterious family secret is revealed.

Will the sins of the father be the sins of the daughter?

As Rae struggles with new friends, a new school and a star-struck forbidden love, she must also face the ultimate challenge: receive a tattoo on her sixteenth birthday with specific powers that may bind her to an unspeakable darkness. It's up to Rae to undo the dark evil in her family's past and have a ray of hope for her future.

Find W.J. May

Website:
http://www.wanitamay.yolasite.com
Facebook:
https://www.facebook.com/pages/Author-WJ-May-FAN-PAGE/
141170442608149
Newsletter:
SIGN UP FOR W.J. May's Newsletter to find out about new releases,
updates, cover reveals and even freebies!
http://eepurl.com/97aYf

Forever Blurb:

S he will fight for what is hers.

What can you do when the people you trust are the ones you should fear the most?

After months of staring down death and escaping danger at every turn, Katerina and her friends find themselves in the last place they'd ever expect. A dungeon. And not the prince's dungeon, either. This betrayal struck a little closer to home.

With time running out and Kailas' coronation looming, the six friends must find a way to make peace with the past to have any chance at a future. Old alliances must be rekindled. Old grudges must be put away. But there are some scars that never fully heal.

Keep your friends close, and your enemies closer. But *this* enemy may turn out to be closer than Katerina ever imagined...

Be careful who you trust. Even the devil was once an angel.

The Queen's Alpha Series

Eternal
Everlasting
Unceasing
Evermore
Forever
Boundless

Chapter 1

It came back to Katerina in little fragments. Not the details, exactly. More just temperatures and flashes of light. Like a series of over-lit snapshots, strewn together on a tenuous string.

First there was the feeling of absolute shock when a troop of soldiers appeared out of nowhere and grabbed Dylan by the arms. He was too stunned to fight them. Too shell-shocked to move. Too completely astonished to do anything other than stand there as the man in charge clamped a silver manacle over each wrist.

Silver.

Vampires weren't the only ones who had trouble with it. Wolves did, too.

His skin had just started to hiss and steam when the soldiers turned their eyes to the people standing behind him. Frozen in confusion, staring on in shock.

Cassiel was the first to spring into action. And the first to be taken down. His hand flew to his blade as he automatically rushed forward in his friend's defense, but something in Dylan's expression made him pause. The two men locked eyes, and the next thing Katerina knew the fae was laying down his weapons, sinking to his knees with his hands folded behind his head.

The manacles went on him as well.

Tanya was the next to surrender. Followed quickly by Aidan and Rose. All three of them could have easily gotten away, but what would have been the point? They had come to Belaria as a united front, to restore the rightful king and take control of the army. They couldn't scatter like a bunch of common criminals. Defeated before their mission even began. More importantly, they could never leave Dylan. Even though he was the one the guard really wanted. The rest were mere collateral.

Katerina was the last to go.

She alone hadn't moved. Hadn't taken her eyes off Dylan for a single second. As the soldier came towards her she was still staring at his skin, watching the way the gleaming silver cuff burned deeper and deeper into his flesh. The same thing was happening to Aidan. And Rose.

How is it possible that they don't scream, she wondered, dazed. *How do they keep quiet?*

It took her a second to realize that someone was speaking to her. By the time it registered, she had been knocked to the ground. She landed hard on her hands, scraping her palms on the rough sandstone, before she was yanked back to her feet. Her wrists bound behind her back. A delicate silver chain tying them together.

And so it was that the six friends were dragged through the street. Cuffed and chained like criminals. Paraded into the city square for all the world to see.

For the most part, Katerina kept her head down. Her flaming hair spilling around her cheeks to shield her from the people's gaze. But splintered images still broke through. A farmer staring in shock, his hand half-raised in the air, holding a horse's lead. A tiny girl perched upon her father's shoulders, pointing curiously and saying something Katerina couldn't hear through the crowd. A pair of women on their way to the market, openly scowling at the band of 'felons' even though they had no idea who they were or of what they were accused.

It was a spectacle for the ages. One that would have been a thousand times worse if the gaping townsfolk knew exactly who was being paraded through their streets—but a spectacle nonetheless. Ironically similar to the gang's recent flight through the midnight sky.

Two exhibitions in just two days. We should really take this show on the road...

The ivory pillars of the royal palace were getting closer, gleaming almost painfully bright in the early morning rays. Every street in the city seemed to lead to the same place, and by the time they'd reached the alabaster steps an impressive crowd had gathered behind them.

"Say something," Cassiel muttered.

Katerina looked up in surprise to see him staring pointedly at Dylan. The two locked eyes and he cocked his head back towards the curious horde of people in their wake.

"Tell them who you are."

It was a testament to Dylan's state of mind that he hadn't thought of this already. If there was trouble within the palace walls, the only chance the gang had was to get the people on their side. But addressing the citizens of Belaria had been Dylan's nightmare for a long time.

He glanced anxiously over his shoulder, looking as nervous as Katerina had ever seen, but for one of the first times in his life words failed him. Not that the guards gave him much of a chance to speak. He only had time to glance over his shoulder, those sky-blue eyes sweeping the crowd, before they rushed him forward up the steps.

An unknown criminal was one thing. But let the people know it was their prince who was bleeding on the steps before them and they could have a full-blown riot on their hands. It was clearly a risk they weren't willing to take.

The crowd remained oblivious. But the people inside the palace were a different story.

There were audible gasps of shock. Hissing whispers and sudden exclamations as the gang was led quickly down the hallowed halls. Men and women dressed in fine clothing, silken doublets and satin gowns, froze in place like lovely statues. Their eyes as wide as saucers. Their mouths agape. Some of them took a compulsive step forward. Most were stunned in their tracks.

I wonder if this is what it will be like if I ever make it back to my own castle. How many people would welcome me? How many would try to resist? How many would just stand there, not knowing what to do?

It was a bizarre homecoming to be sure, but then Dylan had been missing for the last four years. Most of the people in the kingdom had to have thought he was dead.

As they made their way down the mirrored corridors, there were several people he seemed to recognize. Everyone there certainly recognized him. Most looked happy to see him; in fact, several were clearly delighted once they got past the initial shock. And yet there was obvious dissent throughout the ranks. Clearly illustrated in the looks of guilt on specific faces. Of those men who had taken advantage of their prince's absence to further their own agendas. Line their own pockets.

"Where are they taking us?" Tanya whispered anxiously, fidgeting restlessly against her chains. "Dylan, make them tell us—"

But no sooner had she said the words than she got her answer.

The six friends were led through a series of double doors, then came to a sudden stop in what looked like a cloak room. They paused there for a moment, staring on quietly as the soldiers bent their heads together in a hushed conference. There seemed to be some disagreement happening, but before it could be resolved the door opened again and a tall, slender man in dark robes pushed through. His eyes swept over the line of prisoners before turning to the guards in absolute fury—pulling the soldier in charge forward by the collar to hiss in his ear.

Katerina strained to hear, catching only the final word.

"...*cuffs?*"

The guard flushed but held his ground. Staring bashfully at the floor. "We had our orders. Followed them to the letter."

"Orders given by whom?" the man demanded. While he was clearly fighting hard on their behalf, he seemed incredibly reluctant to meet Dylan's eyes. He only ever looked at him sideways, although it was a gesture he couldn't seem to stop. "Give me a name, soldier, or I'll strip you of your rank right here and now—"

"The order was given by me."

A booming voice echoed through the coatroom from a chamber on the other side. The man in the robes and the soldiers froze at the same time, while the friends lifted their gazes to the closed door. It opened a second later and they were led inside, blinking quickly as they tried to adjust to the sudden surge of light.

Katerina's first thought was that it looked very much like the sanctuary of a church. Her second thought was that it looked very much like a chamber she had back at her own castle. The throne room. Where official ceremonies were held, dignitaries were received, and the nobles of the court gathered together each evening to dance and feast.

It's strange... how Dylan and I both grew up in the same kind of place.

Even though she was currently bound by the wrists, the princess stared curiously around the long chamber, struck by each odd similarity between Dylan's home and her own. There were the same long tables. The same crystal lighting fixtures. The same sleek wooden floors, the kind that seemed to echo no matter how lightly you walked.

Maybe our families commissioned the same man to build both. Either that or there's some secret royal super-store that no one told me about...

Two gilded thrones sat on a velvet platform at the very end of the long hall. The same as in her own. One had been pushed slightly into the corner, as if it was no longer in use. But the other was front and center. There was even an empty goblet on the floor by its side.

As they entered the room, the man with the booming voice came into view. At least Katerina assumed that's who he was. Now that she saw him in person, she couldn't imagine such an imposing tone had come from anyone else.

The man was a *giant*.

Standing at what had to be almost seven-feet tall he towered over everyone else, sending a long shadow streaking down the center of the room. His dark hair was closely cropped to his head, and his steely eyes swept over the new arrivals with an expression that sent sudden chills rocketing up Katerina's spine. He wasn't dressed in any uniform, but there was something of a soldier in the way he stood. In the stiffness and precision. That unyielding comportment that made him an invaluable ally, and a terrible enemy at the same time.

Unfortunately, it didn't look as though he was on their side.

"Your Royal Highness. It really is you."

The words cut through the air like a knife. Half the people who heard them flinched, while the others emptied quietly out the door. Dylan did neither. He simply stared back at the man in silence, as if he was trying to place him. Resurrecting a memory he'd long since suppressed.

"Avery?" he finally replied. "It's Charles Avery, isn't it? From the Ninth Militia?"

Much to Katerina's surprise, the giant man almost seemed to blush. As if Dylan had called out some embarrassing detail from his past. He dropped his eyes ever so briefly to the floor, and she was suddenly convinced the empty goblet sitting beside the throne belonged to him.

It took him only a second to compose himself, however. Then he was back in control.

"It's actually Magistrate Avery now." He lifted his chin ever so slightly. "I believe you'll find several things have changed, Your Royal Highness, since you've been away."

No kidding.

There was something about the way he said 'Your Royal Highness' that filled Katerina with an inexplicable feeling of dread. Like the friends had taken shelter in an abandoned cave, only to realize it was already occupied by a hungry bear. The uprising that had killed the entire Hale family had long since passed, and Dylan had never been implicated with the rest of them. In fact, he was so beloved, he was the only one to have escaped the people's wrath. There was nothing technically wrong with him coming home. Nothing this intimidating man could technically hold against him. And yet, the princess wasn't sure that technicalities really mattered at this point.

Dylan gave no reaction to the magistrate's declaration; he simply stared at the man. Placing the ball firmly in his court. Waiting for what would come next. A steady stream of blood dripped down from his wrists. The empty hall seemed to echo with every drop.

For the second time, the magistrate fidgeted uncomfortably. This was clearly not the reunion he'd been anticipating. In his mind, the notoriously hot-headed prince would have made his job a lot simpler. Stirring up tempers and pitting one group of nobles against the other. Entering boldly into the fray with such bravado, that he could be removed with relative ease.

He didn't know what to do with this new version of Dylan. The one who quietly answered questions and never broke his steady gaze. The one who looked more like a handsome young king than Avery looked like a magistrate. The one who was looking more and more ridiculous in cuffs.

"We'd heard rumors," Avery continued, well aware that he was venturing out onto uncertain ground. "Rumors that you were alive. That you'd allied yourself with the rebel camps. Plotting to put Katerina Damaris on the high throne. Is that true?"

"Plotting?" Dylan repeated, his lips curving up into a faint but chilling smile. "As far as I'm aware, Katerina Damaris is the rightful heir to the high throne. That makes her brother, Kailas, a usurper." His voice dropped several octaves, but every person in the hall was hanging on every word. "Correct me if I'm wrong, *magistrate*, but I was under the impression that when the rightful heir to the throne returns home, there is no plotting involved. It's a simple act of succession."

Holy crap.

Katerina's eyes flashed back to Avery. His face had turned an ugly shade of puce. It was a fatal hit, delivered in exactly the right way. Not only had Dylan dispelled any notions regarding Katerina's legitimacy, but he'd validated his own homecoming in the process. Leaving the magistrate no reasonable option but to unchain the prisoners and let them go free.

At least, that's what she thought. But the man apparently still had a few twists up his sleeve.

"If only it were that simple." He shook his head, a look of mock sympathy in his eyes. "But I'm afraid the Northern Kingdom is still bound by the laws that govern them all. According to a royal edict, Katerina Damaris is an outlaw—an enemy of the state. She, and those travelling with her, are to be apprehended and held until further notice. I'm assuming this is she?"

Dylan didn't answer. But for the first time a spark of anger flashed through his eyes. A muscle twitched in the back of his jaw, and for a second Katerina was terrified he was going to tear the magistrate to pieces right there in the royal hall. Then a throat cleared behind them.

The entire group turned to see the man in the dark robes. The same one who'd threatened the soldiers who'd brought them inside just moments before. He was standing exactly where they'd left him, staring at the magistrate as if he'd gone crazy. His eyes ablaze with silent rage.

"Apologies for the interruption. But am I to understand, Magistrate Avery, that you intend to hold the crown prince prisoner? Lock him away in the dungeon?"

Behind him, a group of nobles had gathered. Each one was staring at the magistrate with the same incredulous look. Several looked ready to mutiny right there on the spot.

Avery swiftly glanced at them, then backed down with an appeasing smile.

"Of course not." His voice softened as he motioned for the guard standing closest to remove Dylan's cuffs. "The prince is welcome to stay in his old chambers. All the amenities of the palace will be granted to him for the duration of his stay."

How gracious. Offering him the use of his own palace.

"But as for the others," the magistrate continued, "I'm afraid my hands are tied. Princess Katerina and all those travelling with her must be dealt with in accordance with the royal decree."

At his words, the soldiers who had escorted them inside made to take hold of them once more. Only this time, Dylan, who was now a free man, was standing directly in their way.

It was an awkward stand-off. The prince was clearly unwilling to move. And they were clearly unwilling to move him by force. And yet the magistrate's orders hung heavy in the air.

For a split second, no one moved. Then Avery stepped forward with a smile.

"I understand you must feel protective, Your Royal Highness." His eyes were gleaming with scarcely- contained triumph as he stepped off the platform and walked slowly down the hall. "You've clearly been travelling with these people a long way. You have my assurance that they will be treated with every bit of respect the law allows while they remain in the palace. As will you."

Every bit of respect the law allows? But the law has declared us fugitives. Doesn't that basically strip us of all rights and respect?

Katerina's eyes narrowed into slits as she glared up at the man, while Dylan's fingers curled into involuntary fists. His chest rose and fell with quick, shallow breaths, but when he spoke his voice was just as steady as the moment he first stepped through the door.

"How very kind."

Each word hovered in the air like a tightly-drawn arrow, just waiting to be let loose. However, despite the agonizing tension, he forced his face into a smile.

"But I will not be separated from my friends. Any accommodations you see fit to provide for them will surely be adequate for me as well."

His eyes flashed as they locked onto Avery.

"I am nothing if not a servant of the law."

A whispered hush fell over the crowd as the magistrate reddened once more. He ground his teeth together, clearly at the end of his rope, but the prince had left him no moves to play. In the end, he simply nodded swiftly and snapped his fingers for the guards. "As you wish."

The soldiers swept forward, and the next second Katerina and the others were being pulled unceremoniously to the door. Another whispered hiss swept over the nobles, this one louder than the first, but not a single one of them moved. Not even the man in the robes. They simply watched as the high princess of the land was shuffled off towards the dungeons, her hands bound behind her back. Their own crown prince followed along beside her, pausing only once to glance back towards the gilded thrones.

"I see you've been keeping my seat warm for me." His bright eyes fixed on the magistrate with unnerving intensity, freezing the man in place. "It's a favor I won't soon forget."

With that, the six friends disappeared. Heading off to the dungeons. Leaving the throne room echoing with a chilling silence in their wake.

Chapter 2

It was easy to vent and posture when one was in the brightly lit throne room. It was easy to banter, and glare, and rage on solid ground. It was a far different thing to maintain that kind of composure down in the palace dungeons. Especially when one was on the wrong side of the bars.

"Well, this is just *lovely*." Rose kicked at a clump of dirt as she paced in angry circles around their shared cell. The walls were damp, the ground was slick, and the air smelled as though it hadn't seen sunlight in a long time. "What a hospitable place you come from."

Dylan gave no reaction. He had kept it together only long enough to insist that he be locked in the same cell as the others, then he had simply shut down. As it stood, he was perched on the edge of a lone mattress shoved against the wall. Staring blankly towards the darkened corridor that had led them away from the sunlight and down into the depths.

"Be quiet, Rose," Cassiel chided softly, glancing at Dylan with worried eyes.

Despite the admonishment, he looked as though he didn't entirely disagree. Katerina remembered the way he'd been prepared to fight them free. Remembered that it was a look of warning from Dylan that had stopped him in his tracks. Prompted him to surrender instead.

"Oh, I'm sorry," she griped, flashing him a glare, "are we supposed to be enjoying this? Pretending it's all okay? Maybe I missed the part of the plan where we all decided to get *thrown in jail*!"

"Rose... enough." Tanya sank down beside Dylan on the mattress, rubbing her temples and looking uncharacteristically defeated. There was a distinct slump to her tiny shoulders, and her eyes seemed to have tripled their size in the shadowy dim. "I'm sure Dylan has a plan."

There was an awkward silence as the others glanced covertly at the ranger.

"Right, Dylan?"

It was as if he didn't even hear them. As if he hadn't even realized they were there. He may have played it off well at the time, but now that their audience was over and the key to the cell had been taken away, a part of him was still up in that hall, staring blankly at his father's throne.

Katerina took one look at his vacant face, then stepped up to take charge.

"Of course he has a plan," she said briskly, trying hard to forget his look of complete astonishment the second the cuffs were slapped on his skin. "The confrontation in the throne room was just the first step. To divide the royals. To challenge the magistrate's authority. I'm sure they're all up there, talking it over now. When they send down a representative, we'll make our next move."

It all sounded good... in theory.

But in reality, the princess had no idea what she was talking about. She didn't know why Dylan had been arrested. She didn't know how many nobles, if any, were going to end up on their side. She didn't even know the name of their protector in the dark robes.

As far as she was concerned, the 'next move' could very well be Magistrate Avery turning her over to her brother. She was sure he'd use the reward to redecorate the throne room to his own tastes. Get Dylan custom- fitted with a pair of more permanent handcuffs.

Tanya gave her a tired look, Aidan was blank, and Rose looked outright suspicious, but all of them let the conversation drop as they all retreated to separate corners of the room. Only Cassiel shot her a grateful smile, coming to stand beside her in front of the rusted metal bars.

"You have to admit... it's a little ironic," he said softly. She threw him a questioning look, and his lips twitched up in a faint grin. "When the dust settled on all this, I'd always assumed we'd end up rotting in your dungeon. Not his."

She stared at him a moment, then turned back to the bars. "Thanks, Cass. That's really helpful."

The fae smiled. "Anytime."

Time seemed to move differently so far beneath the ground, but Katerina would guess it had to have been hours before any of them spoke again. She spent most of the time pretending to stare out at the tunnel that had led them into the dark, arms folded stiffly across her chest. Her stance never wavered. Her eyes never blinked. But in reality, she was really keeping a close watch on Dylan.

He hadn't said a single word since the cell door had been locked behind them. He'd simply stared around the room with wide, quiet eyes. Looking far more like a frightened teenager and far less like a future king than he had in the throne room.

Katerina wondered how many times he'd been down to the dungeon before. Staring from the *other* side of the bars. She'd only been allowed to sneak a glimpse at her father's prisoners a few times herself, but maybe it was different for boys. Maybe he'd been expected to take a more active role. Kailas had certainly enjoyed it when the two of them were growing up...

"Okay, so I've got it," Rose suddenly declared, pushing away from the wall she'd been leaning on for the better part of an hour. "We're not going to make any headway when we're locked away down here, so the only option is to escape."

Tanya's eyes flickered up at the word *escape*, showing a spark of life for the first time in hours, but Cassiel shook his head with a slight frown. Dylan remained predictably silent, while Aidan simply stared at the silver bars of the cell, looking decidedly grim.

The fearless shifter was undaunted, tossing back her long hair with a look of fierce intensity.

"It has to be almost time for an evening meal. When they come to feed us, I'll take out the guard myself—Tanya, you grab the keys. There are just two more soldiers stationed at the far end of the hall. If we can get to them fast enough, maybe—"

"No."

Dylan's quiet voice echoed in the cell. He hadn't moved an inch from his frozen position, but it was suddenly easy to see that he hadn't missed a single detail since they'd been led to the cell. Not a word of distress. Not a single scratch on the walls of their cage.

Rose paused, her momentum stalling, and looked down at him in surprise.

"...no?" For a second, it looked like she was going to challenge him right there. Then she remembered her place and lowered her voice to a persuasive murmur. "But Dylan, we've got to do something. You heard that man—"

"I said no." He lifted his chin and looked her square in the eyes. "No one here is going to die. Let alone one of the soldiers. They're just doing their jobs."

Katerina bit her lip as the others shut down. She and Cassiel shared a fleeting look, followed by a quick nod, then he knelt on the ground in front of Dylan, staring intently into his eyes.

A moment later Cass started speaking a soft, rapid clip. His lips fluttered with a beautiful language Katerina had never heard. Dylan glanced at him occasionally, silent and numb, and his tone had just taken on an unmistakably persuasive edge, when the ranger pulled away, holding up a hand between them as if it physically pained him to listen any longer.

"Cass, please, I just..." His voice trailed off as he bowed his head with a sigh. "Just give me some time to think. I hear what you're saying. I just... need some time."

Cassiel stared at him another moment before pushing gracefully to his feet. It wasn't often the two of them weren't on the same page, and it was rarer still that his best friend allowed himself to show any weakness. Neither one boded well. Neither one left them with many options.

In the end, it seemed all they could do was wait.

The girls tried their best to get some sleep, Cassiel and Aidan kept silent watch in the corner, and Katerina sank down on the mattress beside Dylan, quietly holding his hand. For one of the first times since they'd met, even she didn't know what to say to him. But he didn't seem to require her words. It was enough that she just sat there. His fingers were wrapped tightly through hers, and every now and then he would give them a soft squeeze.

It was the only way she knew he was still with them, still aware of what was going on. Then there came a suddenly jangling of keys at the far end of the hall.

The six friends pushed to their feet at the same time. Standing side by side in a loose line across the center of the cell. Shoulders still with tension. Staring unblinkingly into the dark. For a second, they thought they must have imagined it. Then a cluster of torches pierced the shadows, filling the dank little cell with a surge of blinding light.

It was an old prisoner trick. One that never failed.

The gang flinched away involuntarily, wincing as their eyes struggled to adjust to the sudden barrage of light. There was a quiet clink of metal, and by the time they could see, the door was open and the cell was filled with no fewer than ten soldiers. Five swordsmen and five archers. All in strategic position. All with weapons drawn. Each deadly blade pointed directly at Dylan's chest.

"Forgive me, Your *Highness*." The man in the middle sneered as he said the word. Apparently, the magistrate had replaced the more hesitant soldiers with his own. "But this will only take a moment. We just came down to retrieve one of your friends."

The words snapped Dylan back to life and he took a step forward. Eyes flashing. Completely unafraid of the circle of weapons leveled directly at his heart. "One of my friends?"

The brutish sneer on the soldier's face faltered a moment, but he recovered himself quickly with a nasty smile. "Magistrate Avery requires information. Where you've been the last few years. How your path crossed with the princess'. The numbers of the rebel army and when they're planning to strike—that sort of thing." His grip tightened on his blade with an evil smirk. "Since you've been allowed certain... *privileges*, he's decided to obtain that information from someone else."

Katerina swallowed hard and took a step back. She'd imagined the possibility of her capture many times since fleeing the castle, but this was never a scenario she'd anticipated.

Being captured, yes. Being tortured for information, no. What would have been the point?

Once she was incarcerated, the game would be up. She'd always assumed her brother, or whatever other jailer was holding the keys, would simply do away with her and be done with it.

"Is that so?"

Dylan's voice was a dangerous kind of quiet, and despite the fact that he was just one unarmed man a wave of fear rippled through the circle of soldiers. They cast each other quick, sideways glances, but forced themselves to stand their ground. To keep those weapons steady.

"Dylan, it's okay." Katerina lifted her chin, trying to look a lot braver than she actually felt. To be perfectly honest, the prospect of going head to head against the magistrate wasn't what worried her. What worried her was whether or not she could keep control of her emotions until they were through.

The last thing she wanted was to shift into a dragon in the middle of the great hall. She didn't imagine there would be any salvaging the goodwill of the people after something like that.

She took a brave step forward, at least she tried to, but a hand shot out and pulled her back. An iron fist closed around her cloak, keeping her exactly where she was, and Dylan shot her a fleeting glance. His expression said it all.

Really? You really think I'm going to let that happen?

The princess flushed as the words 'unbearably overprotective' echoed back through her head. But in the end it didn't matter. As it turned out, she wasn't the target the soldiers had in mind.

"You—vampire—step forward."

The friends whipped around at the same time as Aidan lifted his head in surprise. He hadn't said a word since they'd been led down into the dark either, and he was taken aback at being addressed so directly now. Every muscle in his body stiffened as his eyes flickered quickly at the swords.

"*Now*, leech!" the soldier who'd barked at him before, barked again. "Every time you make me ask is another minute we'll hold your face up against these bars. Now, *move it.*"

Katerina froze in horror, glancing in spite of herself at the silver bars. Unlike the others, the quick-healing shifters, the wounds around Aidan's wrists had yet to close. From what she knew about vampires, they wouldn't repair themselves until he'd revived himself with blood. And, given their present circumstances, that didn't seem at all likely.

An almost imperceptible shiver ran through his body as he took a step forward. Even now, despite the arrows pointed at his face, he probably could have slipped past them. Even now, despite the grave circumstances, his skill was such that he probably could have still gotten away. But they were here to negotiate. Not to fight. And not to flee. Compliance was the only option.

Or so he thought.

"All right," he said shakily, pulling in a deep breath, "there's no need for weapons. I'm not going to resist..."

He took a step away from the group, prepared to do whatever he must, but in that moment something rather extraordinary happened.

The second he distanced himself from the five friends, they stepped forward to enclose him once more in the fold. The second he left the line, they reached out to pull him back.

And just like that... five friends became six.

"I'm afraid that's not going to be possible."

It was like flipping a switch.

Gone was the remote expression. Gone was the unbreakable silence that had governed Dylan since they were taken down to their cell. The man standing before them now was the same man Katerina had fallen in love with. The same arrogant, infuriating, irresistible ranger. The one who smiled in the face of danger and laughed at the prospect of death.

"You see, as much as I'd love to see you roast the little upstart alive... Aidan's with us." He cocked his head with a smile as playful as it was deadly. "I've grown impossibly attached to him, and he simply cannot leave my side for a single moment."

The room fell deathly quiet. Not a single person dared to move. Only Aidan glanced back with a look of true astonishment, his eyes drifting to Dylan's protective grip upon his sleeve.

The next second, the vampire was pulled back into their ranks. Forever to remain.

"But thank you for coming all the way down to check on us," Tanya added sweetly. "Maybe the next time you come down, you could bring some food."

"We like whiskey." Rose's eyes flashed dangerously in the soft light as she gave each soldier a terrifying smile. "You could start by bringing some of that."

"Except the vampire," Cassiel added practically. "The vampire will need some blood."

Katerina didn't say a word. She simply reached out and wrapped her hand firmly around Aidan's, pulling him even closer. In the darkness, her pale eyes seemed to spark with swirls of liquid fire. The hand still dangling by her side had started to casually smoke.

It was the smoke that did it. Either that or the look on the crown prince's face. For one reason or another the soldiers took an involuntary step back, those fearsome blades wavering in the dark.

"We have our orders—" one of them began sheepishly.

"And I'm giving an order of my own." Dylan stepped fearlessly forward into the gap between the two groups. There was a taunting edge to the words, and if Katerina didn't know better she'd swear he was enjoying himself.

What am I talking about—of COURSE he's enjoying himself. It's Dylan.

"So it appears we're at a bit of an impasse, gentlemen." He cocked his eyebrows with mock concern, looking each one up and down, memorizing their faces. "You can follow the magistrate's orders, or you can follow mine. But I promise you, under no circumstances is Aidan leaving this cell alone. You can take all of us, or none of us. The choice is yours."

He paused a moment, then added:

"We can also revisit the whiskey idea—that's very much still on the table."

Katerina's eyes snapped shut with a momentary grimace. It was a miracle that in the eighteen years he'd been alive, no one in the world had seen fit to cut out his tongue.

The guards in question seemed to agree.

The man in charge—the one who'd threatened to burn Aidan's face—stepped forward with a bristling growl, meeting the prince in the center of the room.

"He's a damn *vampire.*"

His anger was palpable, but at the same time he honestly didn't understand. The magistrate must have thought himself lucky. That he could torture someone the others wouldn't care to miss.

"Yes," Dylan replied with a deadly calm, "but he's *our* damn vampire. And I'm afraid, if you want him, you're going to have to go through me."

For a second, it looked very much like he wanted the hulking soldier to take him up on that offer. His muscles clenched, and his face danced with that hot-blooded anticipation Katerina had seen so many times. Then, as quickly as it came, his eyes cooled with a superior glare.

"If the magistrate wants to ask me a question, he can do it himself." His chin lifted, and the words rang out with authority in the little room. "Tomorrow. In the high chambers."

The high chambers? That doesn't sound good.

Cassiel flashed Dylan a quick look as the soldiers fell back in shock. They forgot decorum entirely and bent their heads in whispered conversation—a sound Katerina took advantage of by leaning over and murmuring in the ranger's ear.

"Dylan, what are you doing?"

His mouth twitched up with the hint of a smirk, never breaking the soldier's gaze. "Isn't it obvious? I'm putting myself on trial."

Chapter 3

"**I**'m telling you, this is one of those things that sounded a lot better in your head."

It wasn't a rare thing to see Cassiel and Dylan fighting. But it was a rare thing when the two of them happened to disagree. The fae kept his thoughts to himself until the soldiers had gone to the magistrate, putting up a strong united front, but the second the friends were alone in the cell he let loose a string of profanities so vile, Katerina didn't need to speak the language to understand.

"And I'm telling you," Dylan repeated patiently, "it's going to be fine. These trials are open to the public. The high chambers will be teeming with citizens from Belaria. I haven't technically broken any laws, and it'll be the perfect platform from which to argue our case."

It made some degree of sense, but the look on the fae's face made Katerina pause. Between the two of them, Cassiel was older and more practical. He'd lived through enough and seen enough to make him take a moment to think, whilst Dylan tended to rush into things head-first, weapons drawn and blazing.

"Yes, that could all be true," Cassiel echoed in the same condescendingly patient voice the ranger had used himself, "...unless you turn out to be *wrong*!"

"I'm not wrong!" Dylan threw up his hands in exasperation, oblivious to the fact that the rest of them were watching the argument with great amusement. "Why do you always assume—"

"Like the time you thought that kelpie was a woman."

"I left the second I knew—"

"Or that time you thought cliff-diving was a good idea."

There was a pause.

"...it *was* a good idea."

"It was a *tiny freakin' pond*, Dylan!" Cassiel shouted. "You hurled your body more than a hundred feet into what turned out to be a virtual *puddle*! Do you not remember breaking every bone in your body? Because I *certainly* remember carrying you nineteen miles to the nearest town—"

Katerina waved her hand tentatively between them, a third-party white flag. "...guys?"

"What!" they both snarled at the same time.

"Are they always like this?" Rose asked in an amused undertone, linking her arm through Tanya's as the two of them leaned back against the stone. "The fighting, I mean?"

The shape-shifter rolled her eyes, letting out a long-suffering sigh. "You have no idea. Although, if they're going to fight, the least they could do is take their shirts off. Hey, princes, show a little skin!"

Katerina shot them an exasperated look while the men had already gone back to ignoring them completely, raising the volume as accusations started flying back and forth from years gone by.

"It wasn't a puddle, it was a *pond*!" Dylan thundered. "How was I supposed to know they'd had a less than sufficient snow melt?!"

"It was a PUDDLE!" Cassiel cried. "And what the heck were you doing jumping into melted snow in the first place? It was the middle of January!"

White flag! White flag!

Katerina jumped in and tried again. "Okay, guys, this isn't helping."

The last thing she wanted to do was be the one who put herself in between two such volatile opponents, but Aidan hadn't said a word since the guards left, and Tanya and Rose had latched on to the word 'puddle' with unmistakable delight.

The ranger and the fae turned to her with identical glares, made a visible effort to check their tempers, then openly beseeched her at the same time.

"Katerina, talk some sense into him. You're the only one he bloody listens to."

"That's *right*, Katerina," Dylan echoed defiantly, "you've got to talk some sense. This is the only chance the six of us have, and he knows it—"

"—don't know why I'm even fighting for this," Cassiel muttered with a glare. "If they don't kill you first, you're going to make a terrible prince."

"You were better company back in Laurelwood Forest."

"ENOUGH!" The princess stepped in between them, holding up her hands. "It's bad enough that we're locked underground without the two of you turning on each other as well. We're getting enough of that from the people outside."

Both men smirked with smug satisfaction, as if her sharp words were obviously meant for the other. She was quick to dissuade that notion.

"Cass, they've already taken the request to the magistrate. It's apparently been decided, so shut up already and get on board."

The fae shot her a look of fierce betrayal, then retreated to the mattress with a treacherous glare. Dylan, who had been grinning triumphantly, was up next.

"And *you*." She rounded on him with little curls of smoke spiraling up from her palms. "The next time you want to make a unilateral decision that risks the lives of all of us, maybe you want to extend the curtesy of *talking to us first*! No one died and made you our suicidal overlord, Aires! If anything, that should be *my* job!"

His smile faded quickly as he held up both hands, nodding in obedient surrender. "I know. You're absolutely right. But Kat, this *isn't* a suicidal idea. It's our only shot."

Her eyes shimmered with lethal fire as her arms folded threateningly across her chest. "*Explain*."

He took a deep breath, standing in the center of the room with five pairs of eyes burning a hole in his chest. Anyone else would have looked greatly uncomfortable but, if anything, the ranger looked strangely at home. He might have been avoiding it for the last four years, but the spotlight was clearly his friend. "Avery has no reason in the world to release us, and enough legal cover that he can easily find reasons to stall and bide his time." He spoke quickly and quietly, like a master strategist who'd already seen five moves ahead. "He's going to send a message to your brother—if he hasn't done that already—and Kailas will mobilize the nearest battalion to take us into custody. The war will be over before it even gets off the ground. With you as a prisoner, the rebels' plans are crushed."

Katerina paused, looking at him shrewdly. "So your plan is to get yourself officially tried and sentenced in the meantime? So you can be executed for treason *here*, instead of back with me?"

Dylan's lips twitched with a secret grin. Clearly, he was no longer speaking to the girl he'd met at the tavern all those months ago. The one who was covered in blood, shaking in the cold, and gripping onto a fairy SOS like her life depended on it. The girl standing in front of him now was calm and collected. Fully in control of herself and her surroundings—despite the fact that she was currently locked underneath the ground in what amounted to a glorified cage. "I've never been more attracted to you in my entire life than at this moment." He shut his mouth quickly when he realized he'd said the words out loud. Clearing his throat, he quickly corrected himself. "I have no intention of getting executed for treason," he replied coolly, hoping very much that undying affection wasn't showing in his eyes. "And neither will you. The second I'm standing in the high chambers, in front of hundreds of witnesses, I can announce my official intention to return to Belaria as king. I can expose your brother's treachery for what it is and declare you the rightful heir of the five kingdoms. Then I can use that platform to mobilize my own army, and together we can round up the rebels and take back your throne."

A sudden silence fell over the room as the five friends absorbed this. After a few moments of standing there, Katerina cast Cassiel a sideways glance.

"...and *what* was our problem with that again?"

The fae rubbed his temples, muttering into his hands. "It's never going to work."

Dylan sank onto the mattress beside him, clapping his back with a cheerful grin. "You've always been such a pessimist. You should try looking on the brighter side of things like me. It's *definitely* going to work, and even if it didn't—what's the worst that could happen?" He looked around the darkened cell with a grin. "It's not like things could get any more terrible than this."

There was an incredulous pause.

"...you call *that* looking on the brighter side?"

Dylan grinned from ear to ear, like a child eagerly awaiting Christmas. "It's the power of positivity, my friend."

The fae slumped lower onto the mattress. "Seven hells... we're all going to die."

THAT NIGHT, KATERINA had trouble falling asleep. She kept dreaming about different things that could go wrong with the trial. That she had to take the stand instead of Dylan but found that she had suddenly forgotten how to speak. That the magistrate started growing at such an alarming rate, that by the time they were able to mount a defense he was over a hundred feet tall and was no longer able to hear them. The worst was probably when the nobles decided to skip the trial entirely, and simply enslave her and her friends instead—making them stand beside the gilded throne with silver pitchers of ale, perpetually re-filling the magistrate's empty goblet.

It didn't help that about halfway through the night, she was awoken by a quiet voice.

"I can feel you watching me, vampire. Sorry to disappoint, but you're not really my type." Dylan's eyes fluttered open to fix upon Aidan's pale face, gleaming bright in the darkness on the other side of the room.

Katerina felt him sit up on the ground beside her, but kept her eyes carefully closed until she was sure they were no longer facing. Then she peered covertly through her lashes, watching the two men survey each other from across the cell.

"I was surprised by what you said earlier," the vampire replied with no preamble, speaking in a soft murmur so as not to wake the others. "I didn't think..." he trailed off. "I was surprised."

"What?" Dylan pulled himself up higher, raking his hair back as his eyes adjusted to the shadowy dark. "When I said I'd grown impossibly attached to you? Or when I told the soldiers I'd love to see them burn you alive?"

Aidan's lips twitched, but his stare was as intense as ever. "Both."

Through the cloak they were sharing as a blanket, Katerina could feel Dylan tense. Through the tiny portion of his leg that was pressed up against hers. His first instinct was to deflect. To laugh it off or lash out enough that the person instigating would take the hint and leave him alone.

But he didn't do that this time. He did something else instead.

"And I..." he pulled in a deep breath, "I was terribly wrong to treat you the way I did when we first met." He glanced at his knuckles, as if they were still stained with innocent blood, before forcing himself to meet the vampire's eyes. "I don't say this often, Aidan, but I'm sincerely sorry."

An abrupt silence fell over the little cell. If Aidan had been surprised by Dylan's show of solidarity before, he was flat-out astonished now. The ranger looked a bit taken aback himself, and Katerina was fairly sure she'd stopped breathing.

But men weren't prone to lengthy silences. They both fidgeted uneasily at the same time.

"You do a good job with her," Aidan said abruptly, his eyes sweeping over the 'sleeping' princess. "It can't be easy."

"No," Dylan actually laughed, gently touching her crimson hair, "she doesn't make it easy."

What—that's ridiculous! I'm the most low-maintenance girl in the world!

...minus the banishment.

...and the royal army.

...and the tendency to breathe fire.

There was a brief pause, then Dylan lifted his head.

"But it's worth it."

Aidan's eyes glowed with the hint of a smile. "I'll bet."

It was quiet for another moment before Dylan glanced up curiously.

"What about you?" he asked. "Do you have anyone?"

At that, Katerina pulled the cloak down ever so slightly from her ear. She was very curious to hear that answer herself. Plus, she was thrilled by Dylan's casual reference to 'having someone.'

"You know, it's the strangest thing." Aidan folded his hands behind his head, a mischievous grin on his face. "Every time I get close to a woman... I end up eating her."

Katerina almost snorted aloud, but Dylan nodded practically.

"That's just basic fear of commitment," he replied. "You've got to face it head-on."

This is why men should never talk about their emotions.

"I'll keep that in mind." Aidan settled back down on his jacket. "At any rate—thanks, Dylan. For what you said. And for the record, I think the trial tomorrow is a good idea."

"Don't let the fae hear you say that," Dylan teased, slipping his arm under Katerina's waist as he lay back down. "But, yeah, I think you're right."

The men rolled in opposite directions, closing their eyes as they fell into a restless sleep. Only the princess was left awake, staring at the ceiling, replaying every word.

So... in Dylan's mind, we're officially together, huh? A little flush smiled across her cheeks, just as it had when she'd referred to him as her boyfriend the first time. *I'm his girl?* Another flush, followed by another grin. *Note to self: NEVER admit that you overheard this conversation.*

Of course, that was around the time she remembered Aidan could tell whether she was awake or asleep just by listening to the sound of her heart...

BY THE TIME THE PRINCESS opened her eyes the next morning, awoken by the sound of heavy boots and clanging armor as the guards returned, she doubted she had slept more than a solid hour.

Too bad, Damaris. It's game time.

She quickly pushed to her feet along with the others, standing in a quiet group in the middle of the cell as the same guards who'd confronted them the night before swept briskly into the cell and started re-cuffing them, one by one.

Something had clearly changed.

Instead of smirking and leering and taking their time, they worked as quickly as possible. Saying not a word. Avoiding each prisoner's eyes. They moved with almost comical efficiency when they were cuffing Aidan, with a look of genuine fear by the time they got to their future king.

"I'm sorry, Your Royal Highness." There was nothing disrespectful about the way the soldier said the word this time; it was infused with nothing but sincere regret. "But my orders—"

"When escorting a defendant to trial, the defendant must be properly restrained at every point during the transfer," Dylan interrupted calmly, sounding as though he was reciting the exact phrase from some long-forgotten book. He held his wrists out in front of him. "Do as you must."

There was a sickening hiss as the silver made contact with his skin, and Katerina couldn't help but wince. She was grateful that at least half of their party was spared that particular torment but, looking at their faces, she didn't know what was worse. To feel the pain, or to have to watch.

Without another word the six of them were escorted swiftly out of the dungeon, through the long tunnel, and back up the stairs into the sunlit halls. Katerina was well aware of the stares and whispers as they made their way towards the high chamber. She could feel the nobles' curious gazes just as easily as if they were using their hands. It said a lot about the legacy of the Hale dynasty that the rogue Damaris hadn't been asked to speak the previous day. But to see a potential queen of the five kingdoms being led in chains through the hall? Right beside their own resurrected prince?

It was almost too much.

Dylan kept his eyes forward and his chin held high. A little trail of blood was leaking down his wrists, staining the floor behind them, and Katerina got the feeling he was making no effort in the world to stop it. Let the people see. Let them know what was happening in their own palace.

A whispered hush followed behind them, and by the time they came to a stop in front of a gothic doorway carved into the wall the whole place felt like it was about to burst.

As long as none of us get caught in the cross-fire. As long as we aren't the collateral...

For the first time, a shiver of fear swept up the princess' arms. In the last few months, she'd found herself faced with almost every kind of danger imaginable, but in a lot of ways this was even worse. It might not be an imminent physical threat, but it was concrete. Legitimized. Long-lasting.

If the council decided to rule against them, if the people watching couldn't be swayed their way... she would be repeating this process again very shortly. In her own family hall.

Bleed harder, she thought, glancing at her captive friends. *We could use the sympathy vote.*

The door before them finally opened, rock sliding over rock with a low-pitched groan. For a second, Katerina stared blankly into what looked to be an empty corridor. A corridor sloped so steeply it looked as though it stretched into the very sky. As she was looking, a man appeared from out of nowhere, hurrying over the smoothed stone, his dark robes swishing at his side.

It was the man who'd defended them yesterday, Katerina realized with a start. Despite having spent the entire night in virtual solitude, she'd forgotten to ask Dylan his name.

"I'll take them from here, Braxton."

He may have been the only person not carrying a weapon, but there was an undeniable authority to the way he spoke, and the soldiers bowed their heads with instant respect. All except this 'Braxton' fellow, who shifted uncomfortably from foot to foot.

"I have orders from the magistrate," Braxton countered uneasily, glancing in particular at the fae warrior and the angry vampire seething at his side. "I'm to take them directly to the—"

"Well, then," the robed man interrupted briskly, "won't the magistrate be pleased that you found a way to expedite your assignment. I'll be taking them the rest of the way. Thank you, gentlemen. Your services are no longer required."

For a moment, Braxton looked like he was about to object. But in the end, he simply stepped aside and let Katerina and the others pass into the hall. It wasn't until he was about to leave that the man who'd intercepted him extended a waiting hand.

"The keys, Braxton."

This time, the injustice of it was just too much. The brutish man stepped forward with a scowl, one he directed at the prisoners while bowing his head towards the man in hushed protest. "Prisoners are to be transferred to and from the chambers under restraints befitting—"

"I know the law," the man interrupted quietly. "I *wrote* the law. The *keys*, soldier."

There was a heavy pause, followed by another sour look. Then Braxton pulled a silver ring from his belt and thrust it into the man's hands, sweeping back up the hallway with a silent curse.

The man watched him go with silent eyes, waiting until the company of guards had vanished and the group of them was completely alone, before turning back to the prisoners.

He addressed Dylan first.

"I'm so sorry, Your Royal Highness." With incredibly gentle hands he reached for the prince's bleeding wrists, lifting a key from the ring to free the silver clasp. "You must know, there are many of us who believe the magistrate's treatment of you since your return has been truly unforgivable. If there's anything I can do to—"

"Leave it on," Dylan interrupted quietly, pulling back his arms. The two men locked eyes for a moment, sharing a silent stare. "If there are as many sympathizers as you say, I want them to see."

Rose twitched involuntarily beside him, looking as though she was less concerned with the sympathizers as with her own skin, but she and Aidan kept silent, adhering to his judgement.

The man lowered the key, looking profoundly troubled all the while, but nodded with silent obedience. He did, however, pull out a leather satchel hidden within the folds of his robes. "At the very least, please eat something." The second Dylan opened his mouth, he was quick to continue, "You'll be no good to anyone if you starve."

That was an offer too tempting to refuse.

With a look of extreme gratitude, Dylan accepted the flagon of water and loaf of bread with tired, blood-stained hands. There was even a small bottle of blood from the butcher for Aidan. He nodded once to the man before passing the wares along to his friends, letting them share in the secret meal before taking part in it himself.

Katerina chewed quickly, taking a few swift gulps of water before passing it along. Who knew the next time they'd receive such basic human warmth. So far, the capital city of Belaria had proven to be as cold as it was beautiful.

"I'm sorry about the blood," the man said quietly, watching the vampire. "I know you probably don't prefer to drink it cold—"

"It's fine," Aidan said quickly, looking surprised the man had thought of it. "Thank you."

When they were finished, Dylan handed back the empty satchel and the man led them on their way. Not a single word was spoken during the silent climb, and by the time they reached the double doors at the far end of the corridor Katerina's heart was pounding in her chest.

"This is it," the man murmured, coming to a brief pause in front of the door. "Best of luck, Your Highness. Rest assured, I'll be there to help you in whatever way I can."

For the first time since demanding a trial, Dylan's look of perpetual confidence faltered. A wave of anxiety swept across his face as a slight tremor shook through his hands. It happened so fast, Katerina half-thought she'd imagined it. Half a second later, he was back in control.

"Thank you," he said softly, squaring his shoulders with a deep breath. "I'm ready to go in."

A moment later, the doors opened. The sloped corridor was filled with light. And the friends stepped into a wide, circular room that looked as though it was perched at the top of the world.

The trial of the century had officially begun.

Chapter 4

When Dylan had announced his brilliant plan, he had done so with all the self-assurance and bravado and fanfare the others had come to expect. There wasn't a shred of doubt in his voice as he lay out the premise. His eyes were brimming with unbreakable confidence as he took them through the details. When he stood in front of the soldiers, he was as fearless as they come.

A chance to lay out his case in front of hundreds of witnesses. To win the very hearts of his subjects. To stand before the citizens of Belaria and take up his crown as king.

There was only one little problem...

"Where are all the people?"

Tanya's quiet whisper bounced off the curved walls of the high chamber, echoing louder and louder with each pass, so that by the time it finally stopped everyone in the room had overheard. A flaming blush burned her cheeks and she stepped backwards, vowing never to utter another word.

The magistrate, however, appreciated the introduction.

"I hope you don't mind," he said as he swept towards them, the folds of his crushed velvet robe swishing around his feet. "I know these sessions are usually open to the public, but I thought we'd do this in private." His lips curled up in a sinister smile. "Due to the sensitive nature of the case."

Translation: You don't want anyone to know what happens here today. You don't want them to hear Dylan speak. You don't want them to see their prince, bound and bleeding.

As if on cue, the cuffs binding them fell suddenly to the floor, vanishing as if the whole thing had never happened. Katerina ground her teeth together, resisting the urge to scream.

Just like Cassiel said... something always goes wrong.

It was a crippling blow. Possibly a fatal one. But Dylan never lost focus. He simply inclined his head with a little nod, eyes flickering to the row of people sitting before him. "If that be the will of the council."

Some of the men shifted uneasily in their chairs, but they nodded in assent. Yes, they'd been officially bullied into keeping this thing under wraps. Dylan might have been the rightful heir to the throne, but he'd been gone a long time. Avery, on the other hand, was an everyday presence they'd learned to fear and mistrust. The devil they knew was better than the devil they didn't.

They were sitting in tall-backed chairs, the kind that seemed specifically designed to be uncomfortable, and were dressed in the same dark robes as the magistrate. The same dark robes as the man who'd given the prisoners a loaf of bread and tried to free Dylan just moments before. The princess realized with a jolt that the very same man was sitting at the center of the line. Eyes locked on Avery. White-fisted knuckles folded stiffly in his lap.

He's the head of the council? Well, that's got to be a good sign—

"Dylan Hale... please step forward."

—or maybe not.

With the quiet composure that spoke to many years of living on his own, Dylan left the others behind and came to stand in the center of the hall. His shoulders were squared and his sky-blue eyes rested steadily on the magistrate. Surveying him the way one might watch a rival knight saddling up his horse for the joust. Taking in the little details. Waiting for him to make the first move.

"The purpose of this trial is to determine whether you, Dylan Hale, have committed an act of treason by supporting Katerina Damaris in her attempt to seize control of the high throne. By acting in direct violation of a royal decree, you have put this council in the impossible position of choosing between the good of the kingdom and the good of the realm."

The magistrate cleared his voice and glanced behind him at the grave faces of the council, letting the words hang heavy in the air.

"As such, it is our solemn duty to deliberate based not only upon... based not only..." He trailed off, staring at Dylan in astonishment. "Pardon me, my lord, but do you find this *amusing*?"

Katerina's eyes flashed quickly to the side.

Sure enough, Dylan was smiling. That same smile she'd seen so many times. The one that said, "I'm a lot better at this than you." The one that made her want to strangle him every time.

"No, Avery," he chuckled, glancing around the chambers, "I don't find *this* to be amusing in the slightest. It was merely your premise. Or lack thereof."

The magistrate's face burned as he ground his teeth together. Either from the laughter, or the reproach, or the casual use of his civilian name. Probably all three.

"Oh, yes?" he asked, trying his best to remain calm. "And how is that?"

A flicker of light danced in Dylan's eyes, and all at once Katerina knew she'd been a fool to doubt him. A fool to be afraid. Ever since she first walked into that tavern and found him, all those nights ago, he hadn't let her down. He wasn't about to start today.

"You're putting me on trial for treason—under the assumption that by my supporting Katerina Damaris' claim to the throne, I'm disobeying a royal edict and endangering the kingdom, is that right?" There was a murmur of assent through the councilmen, and the magistrate nodded stiffly. Dylan smiled again. "But a private citizen cannot act as a representative of the state or be tried accordingly. Surely this council is aware of that?"

Avery's face flushed an even deeper red. It was if his very blood was boiling.

"But you are no private citizen, Dylan Hale. You are a member of the royal family. The only surviving heir of your father, the king. To claim the protection of anonymity would be akin to—"

Dylan interrupted smoothly. "So the council acknowledges that I am the rightful and only heir? The undisputed crown prince of Belaria. My father's natural successor."

The magistrate paled, but the head of the council fixed upon Dylan with a hidden smile, the corners of his lips turning up with a hint of pride. He spoke for the first time. "The council does not deny it."

Dylan glanced his way before turning back to Avery. "As such, I am well within my right to pick sides in any diplomatic dispute. Especially one so obvious as this—when the high prince himself is accused of patricide."

"That is true..." the councilman murmured thoughtfully, nodding to his brethren as he pretended to deliberate. "You are well within your rights—"

"ENOUGH!" the magistrate cried. When the friends had first walked in the door, he thought he'd had them. Now, things were getting away from him for the first time. His temper seemed to be the first amongst them. "You are a HALE!"

He spat out the word with enough venom to make even the councilmen flinch. Dylan's body stiffened dramatically, and Katerina shot him a sympathetic look.

A Hale. It wasn't as bad as being a Damaris, but she felt his pain.

"Why in the *world* would the people of Belaria want you back?"

The words rang along the curved walls before fading into a deafening silence. One that Dylan seemed unable to break. It was clearly a question he'd been asking himself for almost half a decade, and hearing it now, screamed at him in the high chamber, had temporarily stolen his breath.

He was strong, but faltering. He needed a steady hand.

"That's not the matter on trial today."

Under no circumstances was Katerina supposed to speak. Under no circumstances was she to entangle herself in the political dealings of another realm. But desperate times called for desperate measures. And she realized, in that moment, there was very little she wouldn't do for the crown prince of Belaria. She would do even more for the ranger who had stolen her heart.

"It's not the matter on trial," she repeated, her voice ringing with authority, her eyes flashing deadly fire as she came to stand at Dylan's side. "And, as I've come to understand it, *magistrate*, you no longer speak for the people of Belaria. Only the prince does."

The room went dead quiet. No one dared to speak. No one dared to move. Then, slowly, the magistrate began to smile, his eyes travelling back and forth between the princess and the prince.

"She speaks for you... she defends you..." The man's eyes glittered wickedly as they came to rest on Dylan. "Tell me, Your Highness, do you intend to marry this girl?"

Dylan froze for a moment, then his eyebrows lifted dangerously into his hair.

"This *girl*?" he repeated, his face white with rage.

Oh crap, he hit a nerve.

"Dylan, let it go," Katerina muttered under her breath.

But Dylan had no intention of letting it go. Not by a long shot.

"This *girl* is your future *queen*," he said between gritted teeth. "You will address her as such, or I swear to you, Avery, you'll wish you had."

That careful calm had finally cracked. That famous temper had reared its ugly head. It should have left him wide open, but the magistrate seemed no more in control of himself than Dylan was of *him*self. And the prince hadn't actually answered the question.

"And you intend to be wed?" he asked again, even bolder than before. Ignoring the look on Dylan's face, he continued in a rush. "Because I couldn't fathom this newfound return to your royal life otherwise. Not unless you'd secured some sort of promise of advancement."

Not good. Not good. Not good.

"A promise of—"

Dylan took a compulsive step forward but Cassiel appeared out of nowhere and held him back, wrapping a casual but viselike hand around his arm. He muttered something in the language of the fae, and the next second Dylan was in control again. Just barely.

He took a deep breath, squaring his shoulders. "If the council is united in their decision, then I consider the court adjourned—"

"Answer the question!" Avery shouted, baring his teeth as he met Dylan in the center of the room. "Are you going to marry her or not? Because the people have a right to know!" he added viciously. "They have a right to know if you intend to ally their country with Damaris blood!"

There was a pause that seemed to last a small eternity.

Then Dylan pulled in a breath. "I intend to serve Her Royal Highness in whatever way she asks. That is the way a subject behaves towards their sovereign," he added sharply, in a scarcely concealed warning. "A lesson that many in this court seem to have forgotten."

Avery stepped into his line of vision, all seven feet of him blocking the prince's view.

"You *left*," he snarled, and much to Katerina's surprise several people on the council seemed to echo the sentiment. "You just *left*."

Dylan didn't back down. Instead, he took a step forward. Closing any space that remained between them. Staring without fear straight into the magistrate's coal-black eyes.

"And now I'm back."

Avery's hands balled into fists as he slowly shook his head. "Maybe it isn't that simple," he said with soft menace, cocking his head towards the line of councilmen behind him. "Maybe the people don't *want* you back."

It was the only thing he could have said to make any difference. A little dagger straight to the prince's heart. Dylan stared around the room for a moment before he took a step back.

"What is your alternative?"

Wait... what?!

A hushed gasp echoed through the room, and Katerina reached out to grab his arm. He couldn't be saying what she thought he was, could he? Not after all that?

The magistrate lifted his eyebrows in surprise, sure he had heard in-correctly. "I beg your pardon?"

Several feet behind them the head of the council had pushed to his feet, eyes locked desperately on Dylan, silently shaking his head. Cassiel's hand tightened, and he was staring at the back of the ranger's head with such intensity it was as if he was burning a protest into his mind.

But the prince never wavered.

"What is your alternative?" he repeated quietly. "Who would rule in my stead?"

It was in that moment that Katerina realized something very im-portant. As critical as it was absolutely heartbreaking. Dylan actually *cared*. Not just in the hypothetical. And not just a little. He truly cared what happened to his people. Whether or not they wanted him in their lives. Whether he would leave them in good hands. He cared. *Desper-ately*. She didn't think he'd ever realized it himself.

"Who would rule?" The magistrate straightened up to his full height, as tall and imposing a man as Katerina had ever seen. "I would."

The air seemed to drop fifty degrees. A visible shudder ran through the five friends. The same shudder ran through the council. Only Dylan was still.

He looked at Avery for a very long moment, then nodded swiftly.

"Then I'll fight you."

There was an incredulous pause, then—

"I'm sorry... *what?*"

Katerina and Avery spoke at the same time, glared at each other, then turned back to Dylan with matching looks of shock. He ignored the magistrate entirely and turned to the princess.

"You forget, Kat. We're also shifters." He gave her a quick half-smile, as if the entire world wasn't crashing down around them. "And not just any shifters, we're wolves. When the leadership of a pack is in question, there's only one way to settle it for good."

By letting a virtual giant tear you to shreds?!

"Dylan," she said, dropping her voice to a low murmur, "I love you, and I support you, but I'm starting to agree with Cass. This is one of those things that sounded better in your head."

"Nonsense." A bit of that old twinkle came back as he started taking off his cloak. His boots were soon to follow. Her mother's pendant was next. "It's tradition. And I'm nothing if not a stickler for tradition."

On the other side of the room, Avery had kicked off his own shoes as well. It appeared as though he was a stickler for tradition, too.

"Okay, well... is this a tradition you have to do barefoot?" Katerina's eyes widened as a pair of unseen hands pulled her back. "Dylan, what's going on?"

She was being held against the far wall now, safe in Cassiel's restraining arms. A grim look had settled on the fae's face, but he made no move to stop it. Neither did the rest of them.

"I told you—we're wolves." Dylan flashed her a grin before turning back to Avery, a look of sudden anticipation dancing in his eyes. "How did you think we were going to fight?"

THERE WASN'T ANY WARNING. No solemn countdown or ringing of an ancient gong. One moment, two men were standing in the middle of the circle. The next, it was two wolves.

The transformation had happened so fast that Katerina was truly dazzled by it. Her eyes widened in wonder, even as her heart clenched in her chest. She had seen Dylan fight as a man many times, and she had seen him fight as a wolf. But she had never seen him shift—not until now.

She understood why Cassiel had pulled her back. There was nothing restrained about it. No logic or method. Nothing that could be contained.

It was as if Dylan's very body had pulled itself apart.

His muscles tightened, then elongated, scattering his clothes on the floor beneath him in a pile of tattered shreds. His hands curled under and compacted, the nails replaced with a searing row of razor-sharp claws. His face sharpened, then vanished completely, as his tan skin gave way to a sleek layer of chocolate-colored fur, shimmering faintly under the rays of bright morning light.

Only his eyes were the same. A piercing ice blue—the same color as the sky after a winter storm. Just as mesmerizing. Just as deadly.

The entire thing only took a few seconds, but it was a sight the princess would never forget.

"Does it hurt?" she whispered, cringing back into Cassiel's body.

His arms tightened, but it was less to restrain now and more to comfort.

"No, it doesn't hurt." Then his dark eyes flickered to the other side of the room, and his chest fell with a quiet sigh. "But it's about to..."

Katerina followed his gaze, her body tightening in terror. She'd been so transfixed by Dylan's transformation she'd almost forgotten that another man had shifted as well. All of a sudden, there were two wolves in the room. And one was significantly larger in size.

"Cass..." she gasped under her breath. She couldn't bring herself to say the words, but her question was frightfully clear.

How the heck is he gonna fight that?

Never in her life had she seen such a terrifying creature. It was as if the manifestation of all her nightmares had suddenly come to life.

Dylan as a wolf was pure grace. Hard, lean muscles. Sleek, glossy fur. A blinding assault so swift and deadly it could almost be described as a dance.

Avery had a different take. He was power. Sheer, overwhelming power. So massive and encumbering, there was no escape. In a way, he reminded Katerina of her twin's hellhounds. They were approximately the same size—each one standing almost as tall as her head—and there was a hulking similarity in the way they moved. An animal that was too strong for its own good. Thick bands of muscles winding around every spare inch of skin. A neck so thick and large it could break her bones just by swinging its head, and a mouthful of glistening fangs drooling slowly on the floor.

It was suddenly clear to see why Avery had been a captain in the king's militia before he'd been promoted to magistrate. As the beast took another step towards her, its matted black fur hissing across the ground, she couldn't imagine anyone in their right mind daring to stand in its way.

Except for my masochistic boyfriend. Of course, he thinks this is a good idea.

"Cass, do something," she hissed, elbowing him sharply in the ribs.

She may have taken a great deal of secret pride in her newfound ability to step up and take charge, but nightmare creatures from the abyss were better left to the professionals.

"Like what?" the fae replied. He alone hadn't flinched at the sight of the massive wolf, but was watching him with wide, wary eyes. "This is how they do things, Kat. It's the way of the pack."

Avery took another step forward, and the floor trembled beneath his feet.

"Even if the pack is going to be mopping the prince up off the floor?"

She'd said it as quietly as possible, but there was a harsh snickering sound as Avery lowered his enormous head. Standing just a few feet in front of her Dylan swished his tail in annoyance, and she suddenly remembered that, even though they looked like wolves, they could still understand her.

And they could hear a pin drop a mile away.

"Sorry, babe..." she whispered, cringing further into Cassiel's chest. "You totally got this."

This time, the chocolate wolf actually rolled his eyes before turning to look at the head councilman who had just joined them in the center of the floor. There was a distinctly ashen look to his face, but his hands were perfectly steady as he held them up for silence.

"The law states that in cases like this, the fight is to stop at first blood." His eyes flickered between the two wolves. "But I don't think either one of you is willing to respect that."

The black wolf snickered again as the brown lowered his head with a quiet growl.

"Therefore, the fight will stop at first down," the councilman declared. "The first one of you who falls and is unable to get up will declare defeat. If any blow is struck to the downed wolf after such a declaration is made, there will be grave repercussions to the one who inflicted it." His eyes blazed with a serious warning as they fixed on each wolf in turn. "I will not have any death in this hallowed chamber. Is that understood?"

Dylan nodded his head and pranced backwards, bouncing a little in place to keep loose, while the larger wolf pulled back his lips with an unmistakable sneer and stalked away. A moment later the councilman was sitting back in his chair, and all that was left to do was say the word.

"Begin."

It was like an explosion had gone off in the center of the room. As if the foundations of the palace themselves were shaking. Before the word even left the councilman's lips, Avery went charging forward—his feet thundering over the stone tiles, a deafening roar erupting from his lips.

Katerina sucked in a silent scream.

His strategy was as transparent as it was effective. To simply overwhelm with blinding, intimidating force. The problem was... it was absolutely working.

Seven hells...

The high-backed chairs rattled as everyone still standing took an involuntary step for balance. Each pounding gallop sent shockwaves rocketing up the backs of Katerina's legs, and her eyes widened in absolute horror as they flashed to the monster's target. The love of her life.

It was like the world was moving in slow motion. Trapped in the calm before the storm.

Dylan was frozen perfectly still. Eyes locked on the beast charging toward him. Pupils dilated with concentration, and every muscle in his body poised to spring.

For a split second, time seemed to stop.

Then the two wolves collided in the middle of the floor.

The floor heaved beneath them as the five friends were knocked backwards with the force of the blow. Katerina felt the impact in her teeth. Rattling her bones and knocking the air straight out of her lungs. She would have fallen over completely if Cassiel hadn't kept a firm grip.

Her ears were ringing as she lifted her head in a daze, half-expecting to see a giant crater in the middle of the floor. The chamber itself was intact, but there was something vital missing from the picture. In the time it had taken to regain her balance... the wolves had disappeared.

What the...?!

All that remained were splinters of sound. Streaking flashes of color. Like the fight itself had already happened, and they were left watching the ghostly aftermath.

It took a few seconds, a few very *long* seconds, before she was able to make out the shapes.

Avery might have been sized like a lumbering mammoth, but the man was clearly built for action. Not since Dylan himself had she witnessed such unparalleled speed, such vicious agility. And never could she have even imagined such devastating power. The sounds burrowed into her ears.

The blistering snarls and rumbling growls. The high-pitched yelps of pain, followed by the chilling reverberations as the wolves crashed into each other again and again.

Dylan would jump, Avery would counter. Avery would feint, Dylan was there. Ripping and tearing. Biting and scratching. Laying waste to each other with the fury of God's own thunder.

Please, let it stop, Katerina found herself praying. *Just let it stop.*

As she said the silent words, a whole new dimension was suddenly added to the fight. A splash of bright crimson color, spiraling with horrifying speed over the length of the floor. Like a ghastly flower, blossoming before her very eyes.

A wave of it splashed towards her and she hastened to move her shoe.

How they were still standing, she had no idea. How they didn't slip over the wet stones or collapse from sheer exhaustion seemed like a miracle all by itself. If anything, the fighting only got faster. Her ears ached with the volume of the noise. Her knees shook with the deadly vibrations.

At one point a cry ripped through the air, so tortured and deafening that the head of the council leapt back to his feet. His fingers trembled as they began to curl, the same way Dylan's had right before the shift. For a split second Katerina thought he was about to throw himself in the middle, but he held himself back. Letting the men battle it out. Though it was killing him to do so.

He wasn't the only one.

From the second the men had shifted a subtle change had come over Rose. An unnerving kind of focus that seemed to lift her onto the tips of her toes. Her eyes flashed with unnatural fire as she followed along with every minute gesture. Tilting her head, twitching her hands. After a few moments, a low snarl started rumbling deep in her throat. Standing beside her, Aidan was transfixed by the blood. His eyes flashed back and forth, following the fight with blinding speed, but when that crimson pool began seeping their way he actually took a step back. Breathing hard through his mouth. Forbidding himself from looking too closely.

Tanya and Cassiel were a pair of stricken statues. Her eyes were grim, and her hands twitched as she followed along as best she could, unaware that her fingers had curled into a fist. For his part, Cassiel kept one hand laced through his girlfriend's and the other wrapped tightly around Katerina's arm. At first, this had felt like a protective gesture. But now she was firmly convinced that she was anchoring him there, just as much as he was restraining her.

That just left Dylan himself.

There was a momentary lull in the fighting as the two wolves stumbled away from each other, and Katerina was able to see him for the first time. At first, it was hard to differentiate between the two of them at all. Both were limping. Both coats of fur had been stained from their original colors to a unifying shade of red. But then he turned and looked at her with those blue eyes.

A sobbing scream rose up in her throat, escaping through her lips as a quiet whimper. It was a sight she would never forget. The entire range of human emotions, encapsulated in a single look.

"...Dylan."

Their eyes locked.

I love you.

It was just a split second, a frozen instant in time... but it cost him everything.

The second his attention was elsewhere, Avery shifted on a dime and went charging back into the fray. By the time Dylan was turning the giant wolf had already landed on his chest, forcing him backwards as the two of them tumbled to the floor.

There was a horrifying crunch, one that seemed to echo around the curved room, as the bones in Dylan's chest snapped, crushed by the ungodly weight of his attacker. His head fell back with a soft cry, but before he could try to defend himself Avery zeroed in for the kill.

"NO!"

Katerina shrieked aloud as the magistrate began a strange digging motion. At first, she didn't understand what was going on. Then she saw that, with every swipe of his massive paws, he was peeling away another layer of Dylan's flesh. The younger wolf thrashed and screamed but was no match against the sheer weight pressing him down. It was like being pinned by a mountain.

A mountain with razor-sharp claws.

Silent tears were running down Katerina's cheeks. There was a sudden movement behind her as Cassiel raised his hand to the head councilman, demanding that he call for a stop. The man certainly looked ready to oblige, but a second before he could open his lips Dylan spun around on the stones—a blinding streak of fur and blood.

For a second Avery actually pulled back, stunned by the impossible speed. Then, in a magnificent show of strength, Dylan leapt up and sent the magistrate flying halfway across the room. He landed on his back with a muffled cry, his shaggy black fur falling limply into his eyes.

He landed.

And didn't move.

Nothing for a second, then five seconds, then ten seconds, then Kat realized as she let out a huff of breath that she'd been holding.

The fight was over. The battle was won.

A breathless cheer echoed through the friends as the councilmen slumped back in their chairs at the same time. They'd been as wound up as their prisoners, and each and every one stared with unspeakable relief as their prince limped forward.

He had yet to change back. To be honest, Katerina thought it might be too difficult for him at the moment. Every step was pure agony, and every breath shuddered up through a cage of broken bones. She wanted to run out to him. Wanted to break away from Cassiel and wrap her arms around his neck.

Except something even stronger held her back.

He had fought for this moment. Paid for it with his very blood. The moment when he got to stand in the high court of his kingdom and be named its undisputed king.

His entire life had been leading up to this moment in time.

...if only it was meant to be.

An unearthly screech raised the hairs on the back of her neck as a dark shadow in the corner started hurtling towards her. Towards *her*, not him. Unable to defeat the object of his rage, it seemed as though Avery had selected himself a new target.

Time screeched to a halt as she watched him thundering towards her. His steps denting the stone floor of the chamber. His teeth flashing in the sunlight, dripping with her soul mate's blood.

Tanya dove right in front of her, not a single weapon in her hands. She was joined instantly by Aidan, who bared his teeth, as right beside him the air shimmered as Rose began to shift. Cassiel pushed them all away and yanked Katerina back in the process. Standing fearlessly in the monster's path. Not a hope to defeat him. A blazing fire dancing in his eyes.

But in the end, it wasn't their fight.

There was a streak of color as Dylan flew in between them, knocking the giant beast straight off his feet. The stone pillars crumbled around them as the two went crashing into the wall, but this time the crown prince had reached his limit. He wasn't holding back.

Again and again, he attacked. Again and again, it was too much for the magistrate to defend.

There was an anguished cry as he sank his teeth into Avery's shoulder. The older wolf reared up, but before he could make a move those same teeth had sunk into his unprotected throat. The cry cut off in a sudden gurgle, and the giant wolf went deathly still.

Just like that... the room was quiet once again.

Chapter 5

It was a silence no one knew how to break. One that seemed to get harder the longer it was allowed to stretch. The stench of blood hung heavy in the air, the walls were ringing with that final cry, and the world stood still as one battered wolf stared down at the other.

Dylan's chest heaved up and down with silent breaths as he froze in his tracks. Katerina wanted so badly to reach out and touch him. He was standing just a few feet away. But one look at his guarded posture and she thought better of it. She remembered hearing once that the hardest thing for a shifter was coming down from the adrenaline of a fight. It was as if something of the wolf took over, making it that much more difficult for anything human to remain.

If that was true, Dylan was certainly in that place now. A place caught between beast and man. A place that she couldn't begin to follow. A place where wolves guarded their kill.

Cassiel took a step towards him, but a deep growl echoed in his chest. The fae stopped in his tracks. Katerina tried her luck, but his claws scraped menacingly against the floor. In the end, it was actually the councilman who approached. Moving with carefully measured steps. Hands kept in plain sight, as if he'd done this kind of thing many times before.

"Your Highness," he began softly.

The fur on Dylan's back bristled, but he never took his eyes off the slain wolf.

"Your Highness, it's time to..."

The man trailed off suddenly, a look of soft sympathy in his eyes. "Dylan?"

It was the first time he'd said the prince's name, and that alone produced an effect. Dylan glanced at him from the corner of his eye before taking a small step back—away from the body. A second later the man lay a deliberate hand on his shoulder, fingers staining wet with blood.

"It's time to shift back now," he said, quietly but firmly. "There are matters to discuss, and your friends require your attention."

He did well to mention Dylan's friends. The second he did, the prince looked swiftly to the five of them before coming to rest on Katerina. For the second time, the two of them locked eyes.

You did it, love. You got your crown. You saved my life.

The air around them shimmered, and before her very eyes the blood-stained wolf melted back into a man. She stared into his eyes the entire time it was happening. Holding on to that crystal blue. Memorizing the warmth, the kindness. By the time he was human, she was back in his arms.

"*Wait*—careful."

He flinched as she buried her face in his chest, emerging a second later, horrified by her mistake and covered in blood. She'd completely forgotten Avery's gruesome assault when Dylan had been pinned down. The way those serrated claws had dug repeatedly into his chest.

"Oh, my goodness, I'm so sorry!" she exclaimed, clapping her hands over her mouth.

Unfortunately, that did nothing more than spread the blood, smearing it neatly across her lips and chin. There was a quiet tittering in the crowd behind her, and although she thought this to be a rather macabre turn of events the prince's lips twitched up in a smile.

"You're cute as hell, do you know that?"

The others chuckled appreciatively, while the councilman dropped his eyes to the floor with a hidden smile. Only Katerina flushed beetred, hiding her face behind a curtain of hair.

"You're only saying that because I'm covered in *your* blood. Narcissistic bast—"

"Stop." Dylan laughed again, but it quickly dissolved into painful coughing. Without warning, both his legs gave out at the same time and he fell, shakily, into Cassiel's supportive arms.

"You're okay," the fae said softly, propping him up with the utmost care. "I've got you."

But not everyone was so convinced.

"Your Highness, please." The councilman stepped forward, his forehead creased with concern. "We need to get you to the infirmary. Everything we need to do here can wait—"

"No." Dylan ignored Cassiel's helping hands and pushed shakily to his feet. His face bruised and bloody. Little crimson spirals dripping down from his hair. "You've waited long enough." He cleared his throat. "I've waited long enough."

He glanced once at Katerina before straightening to his full height.

"I want my crown."

IT WAS TRULY ONE OF the strangest coronations the princess had ever been to. Not only because the servants not lucky enough to be in attendance were disposing of a body upstairs, but also because of the wide range of people who had been granted places of honor at the front of the great hall.

Cassiel was sitting right in the front—a prince of the fae in a kingdom of men. Tanya was perched smugly by his side. She'd been unable to decide what she wanted to shift into for the occasion in terms of clothes but had apparently concluded that a full ballgown was in order. Sitting beside her was Rose, her dark hair swept up in a graceful swirl atop her head while her multi-colored eyes sparkled under the light of the chandeliers.

Aidan was at the end of the row. At a glance he could almost pass for human, but upon closer inspection he was far too pale. The second it became clear that Dylan was going to be all right he'd discreetly excused himself from the high chamber, fleeing to a place that wasn't drenched floor to ceiling in blood. But he'd cleaned himself up nicely and was watching the procession with a thoughtful look in his eyes.

Probably the first time a vampire has ever been invited to one of these things, Katerina thought absentmindedly. Then she turned and stood with the others as Dylan walked up the hall.

Walked—that was putting it generously.

He limped. Staggered. Hobbled. Whatever you wanted to call it. He was still wearing the travelling cloak that had been lying upon the floor, and the team of servants fussing over him had only just managed to remove the bulk of the blood before he shook them off and pushed through the mighty double doors in the great hall. Head held high. Face set stiffly against the pain.

"Okay... this is getting embarrassing," Tanya muttered as he shuffled past. "An insult to the magnificence of my new dress."

"Would you shut up?" Aidan chided quietly. "I'm trying to watch."

Katerina stifled a smile, keeping her eyes locked on Dylan the whole time.

She understood why he wanted an instant ceremony. She understood all too well his reasons not to wait. The others may have seen him take up the fight for the crown only recently, but she knew better. A part of him had been waiting for this moment his entire life. Whether he realized it or not, a part of him had always been ready. She only wondered if it was worth the wait.

"You're *absolutely* sure you want to do this right now?" the head of the council asked again, the same question he'd been looping repeatedly since the bedraggled monarch left the courtroom. His eyes flickered to the empty seats. The magnificent chamber was all but deserted. The only people present were the ones who'd just witnessed the magistrate's death. "If you gave me a little more time, I could make all the proper announcements. We'd receive dignitaries from far and wide; the people themselves would jump on top of each other just to garner an invitation—"

"Right now," Dylan breathed, taking his place beside the altar. "No more delays."

He'd been waiting four years. He'd been delayed long enough.

The councilman sighed, eyes drifting wistfully over the prince's mud-stained boots.

He had obviously pictured this moment almost as many times as Dylan—the moment when the rightful monarch returned at last to take the crown. The hall would have been done up in splendor. The prince in question wouldn't have been wearing a sling...

"As you wish."

Without another word, he gestured for the prince to kneel in front of the altar on a cushion emblazed with the Hale family's royal crest. Dylan sank down, stiffly, and accepted the scepter and golden orb that were pressed into his hands.

It was a bit touch-and-go with his broken wrist, and in the end he tucked the scepter discreetly into the sling. Katerina pursed her lips while Cassiel stifled a quiet sigh.

Once he was kneeling, the councilman read out a brief litany in a dialect Katerina didn't understand. While it was mainly for the benefit of the rest of the council, who had gathered behind them, the princess enjoyed the rhythm of the language immensely, letting it wash over her like a peaceful creek bubbling over stones. There was so much about this world she didn't yet know. So many languages and customs. Little cultural gems she couldn't wait to discover.

After delivering his speech, the councilman turned to the velvet cushion behind him and lifted a breathtaking crown. It had been carved of a dark gold, crenulated into arching points, and inlaid with a rotating pattern of blue and silver jewels. It looked heavy in his hands.

There it is...

There was a slight intake of breath from everyone present, but just as the councilman turned back to Dylan he suddenly froze. "Your Majesty... I'm so sorry. I'm a fool, I didn't realize..."

Dylan, whose eyes had been locked on the crown, looked up quickly, staring at the man in confusion. "You didn't realize what?"

"This part of the ceremony," the man apologized, "it can only be done by either a member of the royal family or a high priest. We rushed straight down here, I didn't think—"

There was a slight wilt to Dylan's shoulders as he bowed his head. "No, don't apologize. I'm the one who rushed this. If someone ought to have remembered it should have been..." He trailed off suddenly, as if he'd been struck silent. A very peculiar look swept over his face before he lifted his eyes again with a sudden smile. "Actually, I may know someone who can help with that." He raised his voice, glancing over his shoulder at the wooden pews. "Kat? Can you come up here?"

The princess froze for a second, then swiftly got to her feet. She felt the eyes of the entire hall upon her as she slid awkwardly past the others and came to stand hesitantly by Dylan's side.

Up close, he looked even more damaged than before. The bruises had started to darken, and there was an almost feverish paleness to his face. But he was still handsome. If anything, his eyes glowed even brighter, exactly matching the sky-blue gemstones sparkling on his father's crown.

He glanced up at her with a quick grin before turning back to the councilman. "A member of the royal family might be a little hard to come by, but you're looking at a Damaris princess. The rightful heir to the five kingdoms, and the future queen of this land. Would she suffice?"

It was an abruptly tender moment.

As his voice rang out over the chamber, a reverent hush followed in its wake. The rest of the councilmen bowed their heads of one accord as Katerina's friends looked on with a quiet, fervent affection. But none of them came close to Dylan. The princess' eyes misted over when she realized the enormity of what he was saying. The profound significance of the task he was asking her to do.

The head of the council glanced down with a smile, gesturing Katerina forward.

"Yes, Your Majesty. I'd say she would more than suffice."

With trembling hands, Katerina reached out and took the crown when it was offered. It was just as heavy as it looked, but there was a strange weightlessness to it as well. Somehow, as she gazed down upon Dylan's dark locks, she hadn't the slightest doubt that he'd be able to handle it.

She lifted it up high in blessing, and for a fleeting moment their eyes met.

Katerina would never quite be able to explain what passed between them. She doubted Dylan would either. All she knew was that, in that moment, a silent vow was made. The beginnings of a secret promise—the terms of which neither one of them could yet understand.

A little smile passed between them, then she lay the crown upon his head.

What a surprise—a perfect fit.

Another hush swept over the room as, one by one, Dylan's subjects sank down upon their knees in loyal obedience. Only the friends remained standing. Cassiel's eyes shone with pride.

"I crown you King Dylan Alexander Hale." The councilman tapped his shoulders with the tip of an enormous blade. "Ruler of the Northern Kingdom. High Sovereign of the Fifth Realm. Crowned Head of Belaria."

He lifted the blade to Dylan's face, who kissed it gently.

"You may rise..."

INSTEAD OF ENDING IN a ballroom, Dylan's coronation ended in the infirmary. It was a situation that probably would have caused a lot of ironic laughter and mutters of, "Well, we all could have seen that coming," but for once the group of friends was feeling rather subdued.

They waited patiently as the orb and scepter were put away. As the crown was handed off to Tanya—who took it with gleeful hands—and the teenage king was examined by the royal doctor. It was quick, but brutal. Lots of bone snapping, and joint relocation, and hasty sewing amidst harsh objections to anesthesia. When it was all finished, they headed upstairs to Dylan's new rooms.

"This is not too shabby," Rose said with appreciation as they stepped into his chamber. *One* of his chambers. By the looks of things, he'd gotten the entire floor. "*Much* better than the cell."

"Oh, you didn't like the dungeon?" Aidan asked with surprise, kicking his feet up onto a velvet futon. "I was just starting to get used to it..."

That may have been true, but the gang certainly liked the finer things.

Tanya was already mixing drinks into a tray of crystal goblets, Aidan had promptly fallen asleep, Cassiel was raiding the closet for something not stained in blood, and Rose was casually pocketing a golden letter-opener, slipping it into her boot to sell at some later date.

"Please," Dylan said with a wry smile, "make yourselves at home."

They studiously ignored him, continuing with what they were doing, while Katerina slipped her hand into his with a shy smile. "So, how is this going to change things between us?" Her eyes danced with mischief. "Am I not allowed to call you *peasant* anymore? 'Cause I really liked that."

Dylan accepted a drink from Tanya, his lips turning up in a grin. "No, I'm afraid not. If anything, it should probably be the other way around. I am a king, after all, and you're still technically only an outlaw..."

Katerina started to laugh but stopped at the look on his face. It had gone abruptly serious the moment he said the word *king*. Like the reality was hitting him all at once. Like, even though he wasn't wearing it, he could still feel the weight of that crown.

"You okay?" she asked quietly, giving his hand a gentle squeeze.

He nodded swiftly, staring down into the untouched drink. "Yeah, it's just... strange. I guess a part of me honestly believed I'd never get here. That I'd never be standing in this room."

In his dead parents' room.

Katerina realized all at once, and her eyes grew abruptly sad. She should have known there was a reason that he was standing in the center of the room, not really touching anything. She should have understood why he was keeping his hands to himself, his eyes fixed upon the floor.

"You deserve to be here," she pressed in that same quiet voice, giving his fingers another squeeze. "You were born to it, Dylan. You deserve it more than any person I know."

He stared at her for a long moment, that same peculiar look dancing in his eyes. Then he glanced down at their entwined hands with a little smile. "Kat?"

She squeezed his fingers again, tilting down her head to coax his eyes. "Yeah?"

There was a little pause.

"...that's my broken hand."

Chapter 6

That night, Katerina slept better than she had in ages. Once they'd gotten past the initial dungeon, Belaria actually turned out to be a delightful place.

The five friends were given rooms almost as nice as Dylan's, just a floor beneath. Rooms that came with every amenity one could ask for, including a whole host of servants bending over backwards to grant their every request. Giant four-poster beds, silk sheets, mirrored vanities, fresh flowers on every spare surface. Dylan's new subjects seemed determined to make up for their earlier rudeness (aka: death trials and the vague promise of execution) and were turning things around to magnificent effect. From the closets of tailor-fitted clothes, to the trio of violinists that drifted from room to room, right down to the ivory bathtub perched on golden clawed feet.

Katerina made a bee-line for the tub. She didn't emerge for quite some time.

I miss this...

Slowly, methodically, she anointed herself with each of the different bath oils lining the surface of the tub, pouring a little into the water and sniffing delicately before picking her favorite scents and running them at leisure through each strand of her long hair. Clouds of steam wafted up from all sides. Scented with lavender, honeysuckle, freesia, and a dozen other scents she didn't recognize, filling the room with a sugary floral aroma.

When she was finished with her hair, she started on her skin. Scrubbing off the layers of dust and grime. The months of wear and tear. Rinsing and re-rinsing her porcelain hands so many times that she no longer could even imagine them stained with soot or dried blood.

After her hands came her feet. Then her legs. Then her arms. Then she did them all again.

In the end, she had to replenish the warm water half a dozen times, and by the time she finally emerged the sun had gone down, and her eager staff of servants had fallen fast asleep.

She wrapped herself in a silk robe and picked her way delicately across the plush carpet, walking on the very tips of her toes. There was a bowl of fresh fruit on the nightstand, along with a goblet of sparkling wine. A note had been laid atop the utensils, saying that she'd bathed right through the dinner feast—along with the rest of her friends—but that the kitchens would stay open all night if she decided she was still hungry.

She popped a strawberry into her mouth, downed the wine—with fewer ladylike manners than she would have done a few months ago—and plopped down in the middle of the massive bed.

Silk sheets. Did I ever think I'd be lying on silk sheets again?

If she was being honest, a big part of her had to say no. It was a lucky night when it didn't start raining, or when they found enough pine needles to cushion their heads. She'd long since lost the expectation that she would ever again sleep on a bed with no fewer than twelve decorative pillows.

Strangely enough, it was the carpet that was throwing her the most. It felt odd beneath her bare feet. Too soft. Too pliable. Not like the dependable crunch of the forest floor. Or even the sleek but freezing monastery stones. It was a little too... luxurious. It was throwing her off.

She wondered if the others were feeling the same way. She wondered if they were lying awake in their beds, staring up at the ceiling like she was.

Probably not.

Tanya had probably already crept into Cassiel's chambers, Aidan was either passed out cold or stalking off to the butcher's, and Rose was likely to be having the time of her life in any other bed in the palace except her own.

That just left Dylan.

Katerina leapt out of bed the second she thought his name, tying the belt of the robe as she tiptoed over the carpet and peeked out the door. The hallway was deserted. Since they were guests in the palace now, as opposed to prisoners, they no longer had guards stationed outside their doors.

As quiet as a mouse, she flung her damp curls over her shoulders and sped across the stone corridor—hurrying up the spiraling stairs at the end. A massive door was fitted at the very top, but it was unlocked and opened silently as she slipped into the new king's chambers.

It was dark. Every curtain drawn. Not a single candle or torch to guide her way. But her eyes adjusted quickly to the shadows and the carpet muffled her every step. Just a few seconds later she had crossed through all the outer chambers, and was pushing open the door to Dylan's private bedroom, hovering like a nervous silhouette in the frame.

He was sleeping, just like she'd thought. Only, he wasn't sleeping in the giant bed in the center of the room. He was sleeping in the chair beside it.

For a split second, she paused. Staring at him with a tender smile.

Of course he was.

Illuminated by a solitary ray of moonlight, he looked just like a child. His head propped up in his hand, his legs curled up beneath him. The tips of his hair had started to curl with the remnants of steam from his own bath, and every now and then his fingers would twitch in his sleep.

The crown sat on a desk across from him. Looking rather deliberately untouched.

"Dylan," she whispered, not wanting to startle him.

He didn't move. The chair couldn't have been very comfortable, but the man was effectively dead to the world. For a second, she was about to turn right back around. Between the gladiatorial death-match, the impromptu coronation, and the royal doctor's rather overenthusiastic attempts to help, the guy had earned some rest. But then she asked herself a very important question.

How many times in life do you get to sneak up on a wolf?

With a look so wicked her governess would have slapped it right off her face, the princess tiptoed silently across the carpet. Raising her hands like little claws. Biting her lip to keep from laughing. She paused in front of his chair, poised like a diver ready to jump, then grabbed him.

"Wake up!"

It was then she was forced to ask a far more pressing question.

How many times is it wise to sneak up on a wolf?

He awoke with a sudden gasp, grabbing her arm and whipping out a knife before the smile had even faded from her face. The chair fell backwards to the floor as he shoved her hard against the wall, pressing the blade against her windpipe, a low growl rising in the back of his throat.

"...or not?"

There was a beat of silence.

The knife dropped to the floor between them as he released her with a look of horror—his face streaked pale with moonlight, his blue eyes widening in the dark. Just a second later he grabbed her up again, much differently than before. Checking her over for damage, running over every inch of skin with impossibly delicate hands.

"Crap, Kat! I'm so sorry!" How he managed to infuse so much guilt and anxiety into just five little words, she'd never know. "You startled me, I didn't—"

She giggled, and he stopped in his tracks.

"Don't be sorry. That was the point." She wiggled her fingers again, finding the entire thing rather amusing. "How many times was I going to get the chance to sneak up on you, huh?"

His eyes cooled sarcastically as he released her and moved away, bending over to pick up the fallen chair. "Well, I hope you got your money's worth."

"Oh, come on, don't be mad." With a little grin, she plopped down in the center of the untouched bed. "I couldn't sleep. Came up here to see what you were doing."

"...sleeping."

"No, you *were* sleeping." She patted the bed beside her with a triumphant grin. "Now you're talking to me."

He hesitated a moment in front of the mattress, torn between his own stubbornness and his girlfriend's mischievous smile. In the end, the girlfriend won out.

"All right, princess." He climbed to the center of the bed, leaning up against the headboard and lifting his arm to let her eager body wriggle inside. "What do you want to talk about?"

She snuggled into the hollow of his shoulder, careful to avoid putting any weight on the arm with the sling. "I don't know, not much has been going on..."

He chuckled softly but said nothing. Unless she imagined it, his eyes flickered almost imperceptibly to the abandoned crown perched upon his desk.

"What do you think of this room?" She eased into it gently, staring with wide eyes at the corners of the four-poster bed. It was actually quite similar to the one she had back at home. Alike in scale and grandeur, just with a slightly more masculine touch. Things were also designed to be a bit warmer here. The northern kingdom was a lot colder than her own. In the winter, it actually snowed.

"I hate the carpet," he said abruptly, fingers playing absentmindedly with the sleeves of her robe. "You can't hear anyone coming. And it doesn't leave tracks."

She glanced up at him in surprise, then nestled back down with a grin. Of course. The ranger in him hated the prince's carpet. Because the darn thing didn't leave tracks.

"Yeah, I hate the carpet, too." They were quiet for a minute before she tried again. "I'm worried about the vampire."

"Aidan?" It was Dylan's turn to look surprised. "You think he's being treated badly?"

Quite the contrary. The last time she saw him, Aidan was being led away into what looked like a fully-equipped sauna with a trio of three beautiful girls. Katerina shook her head.

"No, I'm worried he's going to eat one of the complementary violinists."

There was a snort of laughter and Dylan shifted her to the side, so he could better see her face. "Okay, let's have it. What's going on?"

"What—nothing." She shook her head quickly, trying to act as casual as could be. How was it that he always saw through her? "I told you, I just couldn't sleep."

"Well, I'm hardly surprised." He bent down to sniff her hair, winding his fingers through the damp curls. "You've probably poisoned yourself, mixing every oil in the five kingdoms." She giggled and tried to pull away as he batted at an invisible cloud of fragrance. "I'm serious, it's a miracle I didn't wake up the second you walked in—"

"Things are different now," she said abruptly.

He pulled back his hands at once and stared down in surprise, a fine layer of tension creeping over his face. She didn't blame him. She hadn't expected to say it herself. But the second the words were out of her mouth, she suddenly realized exactly what had been keeping her awake.

"I mean, whether you wanted it to or not... this changes things."

Like a dream, his words from back at the monastery echoed through her mind.

'How could we be together? Because I can't see it. You want, more than anything, to return to your castle and take your place on the throne. I want, more than anything, to stay away. How could we be together? A queen and a man who spent his entire life trying to bury his own crown.'

Yes, things had changed. One way or another, there was no going back.

"I thought you didn't want this," she said quietly, glancing without thinking towards the desk as well. "When you first told me who you were, you made it seem like this was the last thing you'd ever want to do. That this was the last place you'd ever want to be. And now—"

"And now I'm here," he interrupted smoothly. "Because you need an army."

She pulled back a few inches, staring up at his face. "Is that the only reason? Tell me honestly, Dylan—because I would hate myself forever if you only did this because of me."

He stared down at her for a moment, eyes dilating in the dark, before dropping his head with a tired sigh. "No, it's not the only reason. But I can't..." He paused for a moment, those troubled eyes staring out into the dark. "...this is all just happening really fast."

She lowered her eyes to the mattress, nodding thoughtfully.

Yes, it certainly was happening fast. One minute, they were just a group of teenagers on a rebel journey—eating apples by the riverside and sleeping under the stars. The next, they were standing in front of an altar, presenting each other with crowns and scepters and violins...

"But it's a good thing, right?" Her eyes lifted up tentatively, finding his in the dark. "I mean, I know it's sudden. And it definitely changes things... but in a good way?"

He was quiet a long time, thinking it over. The Dylan she knew would never say anything to deliberately upset her, but he wasn't exactly one to shy away from the truth.

When he finally answered, it wasn't at all the answer the princess wanted to hear.

"I'm not sure it changes anything."

THE TWO SLEPT TOGETHER that night, curled up in the center of the massive bed. It was a strange feeling. On the one hand, they'd slept together a hundred times before. In tents, in prison cells, on a traveling cloak laid out beneath the stars. It was another thing entirely to do it in a bed.

It felt more official somehow. More... suggestive.

There was all the usually shuffling and shifting to find the right position, then his arms wrapped ever so tentatively around her waist. She noticed only then that he'd taken off his shirt and coat before climbing into the bed. She noticed only then that his body was as warm and fragrant as hers.

"Kat," he'd whispered, right before they drifted off, "what are you wearing under the robe?"

Her body had frozen dead still, eyes snapping wide open to stare at the canopy of the bed. It felt like ages before she was finally able to unstick her tongue from the roof of her mouth to answer.

"Um... nothing."

There was a pause, then she felt him smile against her hair.

"Thanks for coming up here."

And with no further ado, he kissed her goodnight.

After that, it had taken forever for Katerina to slow down her breathing. Even longer for her to calm her pounding heart. Eventually she must have drifted off but it felt like just moments later when the curtains drew back, and streams of blinding sunlight stabbed repeatedly into her eyes.

"Rise and shine, sleepyheads! A royal breakfast awaits!"

Katerina bolted upright with a shriek as Dylan grabbed instinctively for his knife. Cassiel was already holding it, twirling it casually between his fingers with a knowing smile.

"You forget—we lived together for years."

Dylan snatched it back with a glare as Tanya continued her cartoonish waltz around the room, pulling open the curtains, twirling on her toes, taking occasional sips of champagne.

While the others may have felt it to be a bit of an adjustment, the shape-shifter was clearly born for this kind of life. Already, she'd located the crown on the desk and was eyeing it covetously, probably wondering if Dylan would let her wear it as he had when they were back in the infirmary.

Cassiel watched her flitting about with obvious affection before turning back to Dylan. "So... you're a king now," he began conversationally, those bright eyes dancing with an amused smile. Katerina got the feeling that Dylan could have declared himself a unicorn priestess, and the fae still wouldn't see him any differently. "How does it feel?"

"Sore," Dylan replied automatically, clutching his recently dislocated shoulder as he hurried about the room, getting dressed. He avoided the new closet like the plague and reached for his old things instead. The rain- softened tunic. The weathered cloak.

Cassiel rolled his eyes and tossed him a pair of boots. "Well, thanks, Your *Majesty*, that's exactly what I meant."

The two shared a quick look, and Dylan shoved him with a playful grin.

"No, it feels... exactly the same."

The others looked at him doubtfully, and he rolled his eyes with a signature scoff.

"I'm serious. It's not that big a deal." In what could have been an accident or by casual intention, he dropped his satchel over the crown, hiding it from view. "Just a means to an end."

"It isn't a big deal?" Rose repeated, raising her eyebrows with a grin. "Dylan, we went to your *coronation* yesterday. But maybe he doesn't remember," she added suddenly, turning with mock concern to the others. "He lost a lot of blood..."

"If it's any consolation," Aidan said supportively, "I also think it wasn't a big deal."

Tanya tossed a grape at him. She was perched on a velvet cushion with all the bearing of an evil queen. "...peasant scum."

"Relax," Dylan insisted, walking over to the balcony to let in some fresh air. "The entire thing took about five minutes and we were the only people there. It's not like anybody knows—"

Of course, that's when Tanya opened the door to the balcony and the screams of a thousand people rushed inside.

Chapter 7

The balcony door shut as quickly as it had opened, leaving the six friends standing in stunned silence on the other side. For a second, nobody moved. Then Aidan leapt back with such blinding speed it would have been comical if it wasn't so serious.

"Are they cheering or screaming?" he demanded, angling himself defensively behind a velvet chair. His eyes were wide and tense, and when the doorknob rattled he jumped again.

"How the he-heck could word have gotten out so quickly?" Dylan murmured, staring at his friends in a sort of daze. "I thought it would take at least—"

"What does it matter?" Rose asked impatiently. "It's not like they weren't going to find out, Dylan. You're their *king* now. Go out and say something. Make a speech!"

Tanya seemed to think this was a great idea. She'd already unearthed the crown from behind the satchel and was practicing her royal wave. On the other side of the room the door to the chamber shook again, although no one seemed to notice except the vampire.

"Are they cheering or screaming?" he pressed all the more urgently. Katerina shot him a questioning look, and he rolled his eyes. "Believe me, when you've been chased out of town by a mob as many times as I have, you learn to appreciate the difference."

The entire room was awash with nervous energy. Some excited. Some incredulous. Some just plain scared. The vibrations from the crowd rattled the panes of glass in the balcony doors; the girls drifted towards it, while the boys melted back. Aidan was still angled behind a chair, Katerina was desperately wishing that she was wearing something more beneath the robe, Rose and Tanya were already rehearsing their speeches for imaginary state dinners, and Dylan was staring towards the courtyard with something close to dread.

"Hey," Cassiel started, approaching him carefully, standing near the back of the group. He alone had been neither surprised nor fazed by the onslaught of sound. His only focus was on how it might affect his best friend. "You okay? You know, Rose is right. This *was* going to get out eventually—"

"...cheering or screaming..."

"Yeah, but *later*." Dylan sucked in a sharp breath, cringing away from the sound. "Sometime after we had already—"

The door finally burst open, and the head of the council walked inside. For a second, everything was comically still. The six friends stared at him, and he stared at their frozen position in front of the window. Then his eyes fell upon Dylan, and he swept forward with a warm smile.

"Your Majesty." He sank into a low bow, then straightened back up. "I came to warn you, but I see you've already found them. When news of your return and coronation got out, people from all over the countryside swarmed into the city to celebrate and pay their respects."

"Thank the maker..." Aidan sank into the nearest chair, looking pale. "...*cheering*."

Dylan cast the vampire a quick look before turning his back deliberately on the window. As if simply not seeing them would make the scores of people disappear. "Yes, but how did news get out so quickly? I wasn't planning on..." He trailed off, running a nervous hand through his messy hair. "Do they expect me to make some kind of speech? Because I don't—"

The councilman held up a hand and shook his head, stopping the little panic attack in its tracks. "Not in the slightest. They are merely here to show their support. However, it might be a kind gesture to stand out on the balcony and wave. Let them get a look at you—it has been years, after all." His eyes drifted discreetly down at his king's attire. The mud-stained boots, seasoned cloak, and rebel blades—all of which looked as though they had seen better days. "Were you not able to find anything to your liking in the closet, Sire? I'd be happy to send in the tailor."

At the word *tailor*, Dylan clearly reached his limit.

"I don't think that will be necessary." Cassiel stepped in quickly to intervene, ushering the man away with a gracious smile. "He'll step out and greet the people then, unless I'm mistaken, we'd all love a chance to go down and tour the royal armory."

Royal armory effectively cancelled out *tailor*.

Dylan's eyes lit up for the first time since his strange awakening that morning and he turned hopefully to the councilman, looking a bit like a child hovering in front of a toy store. For his part, the councilman took his cue like a champion and nodded swiftly.

"Of course, I'd be happy to escort you there myself." He shot Cassiel a grateful look as Dylan hastily tidied himself up in front of a mirror. "I think you'll find we've made several changes since you've been away. All of which will be to your liking."

It was like he'd taken some kind of testosterone sedative. Dylan carefully removed his own battered weapons and lay them lovingly upon the comforter. He knocked a bit of mud off his boots, and even switched out his cloak for another, before returning to Katerina with a smile.

"Will you come with me?" he asked, holding out his hand.

She hesitated, glancing out at the screaming horde, before taking a step back. "No, I think this is probably something you should do on your own..."

His face fell ever so slightly, though his hand stayed raised between them. "Why? Come on, Kat, just come with me. Then we can look at the new weapons," he added with a conspiratorial grin.

She rolled her eyes and gathered the robe tighter around her. Was he really going to make her say it in front of the room? In his weapon-induced haze, had he really forgotten?

"Dylan..." Her face flushed bright red as she stood up on her tip-toes, whispering hastily into his ear. "I can't go out there like this. I've got nothing on under the robe..."

Why even bother trying to whisper in a room full of shifters?

Cassiel grinned, Tanya buried her face with a snort, Aidan rolled his eyes, and Rose shot her a look of shameless approval. Only Dylan froze in sudden recognition before his eyes twinkled and he smiled a mischievous smile. A smile that earned him an instant slap.

"It's not funny."

The councilman bowed his head for a moment before looking up with a carefully contained expression. "Your Highness, perhaps I might be of assistance." Without another word, he snapped his fingers and the door opened. A waifish girl slid inside. One with pale skin and eyes that stayed trained on the floor. "Anna, would you run downstairs and fetch some of the princess' clothes?"

Oh, just kill me now...

Katerina closed her eyes in a pained grimace as the rest of them continued their shameless congratulations for something that had never come to be. Less than a minute later, the girl returned and gestured shyly for the princess to follow her into the private dressing room. She did so with great relief, leaving her friends behind, laughing loudly in her wake.

"Thank you so much for this." She gratefully took the bundle of clothes from the girl's slender fingers, forgetting everything except the urgent need to dress. "You really have no idea how intolerable the lot of them can be. Especially when they're all together—"

"Milady, please." There was a gentle tug as the girl took the dress the princess had been in the process of unfolding back into her own hands. "Allow me."

Katerina froze perfectly still. Embarrassed by her own mistake. Crashing back down to reality. Stunned by just how much the innocuous little moment threw her off track.

Milady.

She used to hear the word a thousand times a day back at the castle. She'd grown as accustomed to it as she had her own name. Now, it felt strange and pretentious to her ears.

The dress slipped over her head—a beautiful gown of deep sapphire silk—as she stood there like a statue. Feeling a bit as though she'd finally come home, only to realize that someone else was living in her room. It was as familiar as it was foreign, leaving her tense and quiet in its wake.

Anna hardly noticed.

She went about her work with silent efficiency, just as the maid-servants were trained to do back in Katerina's own home. Her fingers blurred with speed as she laced a silk corset expertly up the princess' back, then she turned her attention to the stockings, holding the top of them open and waiting for the princess to step inside.

Katerina followed along like a doll. Lifting her arms obediently. Sucking in her breath when she was supposed to. Going through the puppet-like motions, as she had her entire life.

But she stopped when she got to the stockings.

"I don't think I'll be wearing those."

The corset was bad enough. She didn't want to imagine the looks on the others' faces if she walked back into the room with patterns of swirling lace inching up her thighs...

It's all going to rip apart anyway the next time I become a dragon...

"Are you sure, milady?" The young girl's face tightened; she was clearly unsure what to do if the routine suddenly deviated from the rules. "Protocol dictates that—"

"I know what the protocol says," Katerina replied quickly. "And you don't have to call me 'milady'," she added, knowing the words would fall on deaf ears. "It's Kat."

The girl looked at her like she'd spoken another language, then nodded swiftly and backed away. A second later she was gone, leaving the princess staring at a perfect stranger in the mirror.

Is that really me? It feels like someone I knew so long ago...

She scarcely recognized her reflection. It was like staring at some distant acquaintance. A third cousin, once removed. The kind of person whose name you should probably remember, but for whatever reason it always freezes on the tip of your tongue.

Her fiery red hair, which had been pulled back most days in a simple leather band, had resisted Anna's efforts for only a moment before falling back into its customary waves. Her cheeks, which had grown tan and angular over the last few weeks, had been brushed with the slightest bit of rouge, and her lips had been smeared with an accompanying shade of red.

At some point during the process, the maid had discreetly slipped a series of delicate jeweled bracelets around the princess' thin wrists. Gifts from the palace. Each one of them probably costing more than the entire food budget of a camp like Pora for a month.

Her eyes shone like little stars beneath a dusting of shimmer. Her skin was soft and bright.

All in all, she supposed that she looked like her old self again. Like a princess, not a rebel fighter. Like a woman with a kingdom, a woman about to be made queen.

Then why did a solitary question keep looping through her mind?

There are no belt loops... where am I going to put my knife?

Her shoulders fell with a quiet sigh as she went back to rejoin the others—understanding for the first time the impulse that had made Dylan hide the crown beneath his bag.

The little transformation had only taken a few minutes, and the crowd was still going strong by the time she walked back into the room. Their voices rose and fell against the glass like a wave, sending vibrations up through the floor and rattling the crystal goblets lined across the vanity. Her sudden reappearance prompted a few casual smiles from her friends and a nod of approval from the councilman. But if Katerina was hoping to get a reaction from Dylan, she was going to be disappointed.

"Finally. Let's go."

Without giving her a second glance he grabbed her hand, pushed open the door, and half-dragged her out onto the balcony. It was clearly one of those 'If I don't go now, I'm going to lose my nerve' moments and, given the reaction that followed, Katerina could hardly blame him.

The second their new king emerged through the ivory doors, the people gathered on the ground below simply lost their minds. There was no other way to describe it.

Katerina had never seen such fervor. Such ardent adoration for a person they loved from a distance but had never actually met. The sheer volume shocked her ears, made her eyes water, and triggered an automatic grimace that she was quick to turn into a smile as she raised her hand in a wave.

It's not like I haven't been to one of these things before. The least I can do is put on a good show.

It wasn't like this was his first time, either but, standing on the balcony beside her, Dylan was completely frozen. The man who had charged a giant, the man who'd ripped an arrow out of his leg just to outfox the royal army, the same man who charged bravely into battle, who had never once shrunk away from a fight... he found himself suddenly unable to move.

"Kat..."

She could barely hear his voice over the noise. If she hadn't been watching out of the corner of her eye, she would never have known that he'd spoken at all.

"Kat, I can't—"

"Yes, you can," she said firmly, keeping that smile plastered on her face.

With a deliberate hand she reached across and took him by the wrist, raising his arm as the crowd below went wild. His muscles tensed as he flinched away, probably wishing he was back in the relative solitude of the dungeon, but after a second he recovered himself enough to wave. Then to smile. Then to lift his other hand to the deafening applause that followed.

"See?" By the age of nine, Katerina had perfected the art of speaking through her teeth. "It's a piece of cake. Really, *really* loud cake."

He tried to laugh, but the sound caught in his throat. Instead he turned to give her a grateful look, then froze dead still once again. His eyes widened, and his lips parted in visible surprise. A look of complete wonder flitted across his face, and after a moment he finally met her eyes.

"You look stunning."

A delicate blush washed across the princess' cheeks as she lowered her hand to the stone railing. Comments like that were the only thing that made corsets remotely bearable.

"While you... are still covered in dirt."

He broke out of his trance and glanced at himself self-consciously. Only then did he seem to notice the difference between them. The effort she had made, that he had clearly not. At the same time, he saw the bracelets sparkling on her wrists.

"Stealing, are we?" His eyebrows cocked with a sarcastic smile. "You know, Katerina, it's bad form when you repay the hospitality of your host by turning into a petty thief."

She flipped back her hair with a casual shrug, letting the jewels sparkle in the light.

"I'll do as I wish. You see, this may be your kingdom, Dylan, but I think we both know it's really just an extension of *my* kingdom. The way I figure—everything in it belongs to me."

"Is that right?" He cocked his head with a devilish smile, one that made her suddenly grateful for the thousands of witnesses. "Everything here belongs to you?"

"That's right," she answered flippantly, playing with fire but loving every second of it.

There was a pause.

"Does that include me?"

The princess sucked in an inaudible breath.

The old Katerina would have blushed to high heaven. The old Katerina might have considered jumping off the balcony just to avoid having to answer. But no matter how much that girl in the mirror might look like her, the old Katerina was gone. And she wasn't coming back.

"I seem to remember a certain vow you made in the high chamber." She lifted her chin and looked at him with a steady smile. "A vow to serve your queen in whatever way she asked."

It was a challenge. And a subtle invitation. All at once.

A strange series of expressions flitted across Dylan's face. First, he was surprised. Then impressed. Then hesitant. Then vaguely predatory, in a way that sent shivers up Katerina's spine.

"And what is it you would ask, my queen?" His blue eyes darkened with a scorching heat as they gazed down into hers. "Are we talking money? Land? Or is this more of a personal favor?" The corners of his mouth curved up, and her stomach tightened into knots. "A more... intimate request?"

The air between them shot up a thousand degrees as their gazes locked.

They stared for a suspended moment, neither one backing down, neither one surrendering a single inch. Then, with deliberate nonchalance, Katerina turned back to the adoring crowd.

"I'm keeping my options open." Her wrist jingled as she lifted it up to wave, flashing him a mischievous smile at the same time. "Right now, all I want is the bracelets..."

KATERINA AND DYLAN stood there waving until she thought her ears were about to bleed, at which point they retreated inside. They hadn't spoken a word to each other since the comment about the bracelets, but occasionally she'd see his eyes drift towards her, fighting back a smile.

By the time they returned, their friends had been forced—or gleefully volunteered—to undergo a similar transformation as the princess had herself.

Rose was clean, and styled, and laced up in a corset similar to Katerina's—her dark hair spilling in little tendrils down her back. It was the least skin the princess had ever seen her show, a fact that seemed to make her increasingly uncomfortable. Hardly a few seconds would go by before her fingers drifted up again to her high collar, tugging restlessly at the lace seam.

Tanya's shaved mohawk seemed to have rather baffled the royal hairdressers, but in the end they fitted her with a diamond circlet—making her look like some sort of gladiatorial princess. An appearance that was greatly enhanced by the shimmering silver gown clinging to her thin frame.

Both Aidan and Cassiel had been caught in the same trap, but while the girls were styled to look as all girls of the court do, they'd been allowed to keep their cultural differences. The fae was wearing an ivory tunic with a cloak of pale grey. His white-blond hair fell loose around his collarbones, and for the first time since Katerina had met him at the inn all those nights ago there wasn't a perpetual layer of someone else's blood coating the back of his hands.

While the fae was all lights, the vampire was all darks. Dark pants, shirt, jacket. Even a pair of dulled leather boots that Aidan seemed to particularly enjoy. The colors suited him. Highlighted the paleness of his skin, the rich contrast of his hair. They drew attention to the almost absurd handsomeness of his face and made his eyes stand out like roving jewels, glittering in the light.

Dylan was quick to tease. Then he was caught as well.

The man might have been able to command an army, but he was no match against his own staff. The second he returned from the balcony he was whisked away by a team of no fewer than five people, and emerged several minutes later looking not at all like the ranger who had left.

He looked like a king.

A young king. A restless and mischievous king. A king who'd rather be playing death games with the royal army than fidgeting in a silken doublet. But a king nonetheless.

Okay... seriously?! Give me a break!

Katerina's mouth fell open as she stared in blatant shock across the room. She might have spent the better part of three months with the man, but the sight of him now made her downright dizzy. Stole the breath right out of her lungs.

How can one person be so beautiful? How is it possible to look like that all by himself?

The women seemed to agree.

For one of the first times ever, Tanya was staring at him in stunned silence. There was no sarcastic comment, no teasing little quip that came to her lips. Rose, on the other hand, stared at Dylan for only a moment before turning to Katerina, obviously debating whether or not to ask if the princess would be willing to share.

The men were not so easy to impress.

Cassiel simply glanced at his friend with bored disinterest before pouring himself a drink, while Aidan took a step towards him, looked him up and down, then smirked.

"Nice coat."

The moment shattered, and Dylan tugged at the embroidered sleeves with a scowl. "Why is it that you were given normal clothes, while I look—"

"*Hot*," Tanya interjected.

"*Insanely* hot," Rose clarified.

Katerina needed a second more to regain her voice. But she did manage an indifferent shrug. "...you look all right."

The two locked eyes, and the freshly anointed king actually blushed.

"Seriously," Aidan looked him up and down with a grin, unable to resist pressing the matter further, "I'm actually considering taking up croquet. Just being in such close proximity."

"This wasn't my fault," Dylan fumed, seconds away from ripping the unfamiliar clothes to pieces. "I didn't ask for it—"

"Really?" Cassiel interjected, tilting his head with a crooked smile. "Because I seem to recall you saying, '*I want my crown*'. It was rather infantile, in fact..."

Dylan's blue eyes narrowed into slits. "I can still kill you, you know. No matter what I happen to be wearing."

The fae cocked his head, looking him up and down appraisingly. "By the looks of things, I'd say you'd sooner invite me to brunch... but I admire your confidence."

"Okay, enough." In an act of supreme charity, Katerina decided to intervene. It helped matters greatly that the man she was defending happened to look like a fairytale prince. The kind who recused the princess, but only after he took her to bed. "I'm all for teasing just as much as the next girl but, lest you forget, we're about to go down to the *armory*, which I'm sure is surrounded by a host of guards. All of whom are duty-bound to *kill* you if this one snaps his fingers."

Dylan's glare melted into the world's smuggest smile.

Kat wasn't finished. "Even if he does look like something you'd find on top of a cake."

DESPITE THE TEASING, the walk down to the armory was a silent one. None of the friends spoke to each other at all except for Tanya, who stretched onto her toes for a moment and bit a stone sewn into the fabric on Dylan's arm. When he turned to her in shock, she retreated with a casual shrug.

"...just seeing if it was real."

News of their visit had obviously spread, because by the time they made their way across the palace to where the weapons were held a large contingent of soldiers was stationed outside. Dylan looked at them in surprise before turning with a pointed stare to Aidan.

The vampire flashed him a nervous thumbs-up.

Katerina, on the other hand, was absolutely fascinated. Not by the soldiers—she had seen those a million times before. But because of what these particular soldiers happened to represent.

These are on our side.

Soldiers—just like the ones they'd been running from, except these were wearing silver and blue. Soldiers—just like the ones who'd been hunting them, except these would answer to Dylan, and would, by extension, answer to her.

For the first time, the sheer magnitude of what was happening hit her all at once. No longer was she a girl on the run, in the company of strangers, just trying to stay alive. No longer were her plans limited to a single rebel camp and a circle of five people. From the moment Dylan had taken that crown, everything had escalated. From the moment he took that crown, everything changed.

These men were hers now. The beginning of her army. Willing to fight for her. Willing to die if it was deemed necessary. What had started as a desperate fight for survival had somehow turned into an all-out war. She would be marching with these men back to her castle. Countering her brother's army with one of her own.

There would be death. A lot of death.

But maybe, when the dust finally cleared, things would also be set right.

"—just in from Calgary. The newest in the battalion. But when we heard you were back..."

Katerina tuned back in to see that the ranking officer had appeared and was speaking to Dylan with an awed sort of reverence. There were a few men on either side who were craning to get a better look, but for the most part their discipline was extraordinary. Spines stiff and rigid. Eyes staring straight ahead. Never blinking. Never deviating.

Not even when Tanya stepped experimentally on one of their feet.

"Newest in the battalion, huh?"

Dylan had been expecting a break. The chance to lock himself away with his friends and play with a room full of toys designed to take a man's head off in about nineteen different ways. The last thing he wanted was to give an unscripted speech.

"That's right, Sire. Out of training for only three weeks."

Dylan nodded uncomfortably and made to stick his hands into his cloak. Then he realized he wasn't wearing his cloak and dropped them awkwardly to his sides. The friends grinned, but the man he was speaking to never noticed. He was as enraptured as the first moment the king arrived.

Fortunately, a sudden movement attracted Dylan's attention and his eyes shot down the row to a young man standing at the very end. This one was small—much smaller than the others—and had accidentally tripped forward in the hopes of getting a better look at the king's face.

Dylan's lips turned up in a smile as he took an automatic step, then gestured the man forward, eyes fixing with great interest on the three-pronged blade hanging by his side. He stared for a moment with open jealousy before remembering he had the right to examine the thing himself.

"May I?" he asked, holding out his hands.

The soldier stared open-mouthed for a second before hurrying to comply. With trembling hands, he unhooked the blade and lay it carefully across Dylan's palms.

Dylan wasn't so careful.

"This is incredible," he murmured, flipping the thing around with such speed that the soldier who gave it to him took an automatic step back. "Perfectly balanced, nice grip..."

He gave it an expert slice through the air, listening with satisfaction to the deadly hiss that followed, before handing it back with a smile.

"I may have to get one of those for myself before all the fighting begins."

The soldier laughed a little breathlessly, staring down at the blade as though he was going to have it framed. "Oh, there won't be any need for that, Your Majesty."

Dylan's smile froze on his face as he looked up in surprise. "And why is that?"

The soldier glanced hastily between his king and his commanding officer, terrified that he'd made some kind of mistake. "I only meant... you won't be anywhere near the fighting, Sire."

A shadow of confusion passed across Dylan's face, but before he could open his mouth to ask the officer stepped between them with a respectful smile.

"You have been crowned king, my lord. We aim to keep you safe. As far away from the battle as possible. There will be no need to bring a blade."

In his mind, the words were perfectly reasonable. Uttered with nothing but the appropriate respect. He could have no way of knowing the reaction they would trigger. Of the dark seed he'd inadvertently planted deep in the young king's mind.

But Katerina saw it. Clear as day.

Like I said... this changes things.

When Dylan woke her before dawn the next morning, she shouldn't have been surprised.

Chapter 8

First hint: he came in through the window, not the door.

Second hint: he was wearing his old clothes; the doublet was in a pile in the closet.

Third hint: he refused to speak in anything louder than a whisper.

"Kat. Wake up."

She rolled over in a cocoon of blankets, feeling temporarily lost in the vast bed. The early morning sun was just starting to peek in through the curtains, and after blinking several times she was able to make out the silhouette of the man sitting on the edge of the mattress.

"Dylan?" He nodded, and her face screwed up into a scowl. "What the heck are you doing here? It has to be, like, six in the morning."

"Five," he answered shortly. "Come on. You've got to get up."

If they'd been out in the woods, she might have listened. If they'd been out in the woods, she might have been worried about a bear. But while some parts of a return to royal life might chafe, the luxurious bed was certainly not one of them. Neither was the concept of sleeping in.

"Be gone, you psycho. Before I call my guards."

His face was still shadowed, but she could have sworn he rolled his eyes.

"They're actually my guards, but way to embrace the stereotype." A hand came up and ripped off her top layer of blankets. "Come *on*, I said. We're in a hurry."

Another blanket ripped away. Then another. Then another. Then he suddenly paused.

"How deep are you buried in this thing?

Her lips curled into a smirk.

"You'll never find me..."

"*Katerina.*"

92

Her eyes opened then, and with great reluctance they focused on his face. It was then she fully noticed the clothes, then she registered the whisper. And it was then she saw the window hanging open on the ledge. Her heart quickened as her stomach sank with a feeling of dread. "Dylan, what are you doing here?"

His face was rigid and set. No hint of a twinkle in those ice-blue eyes. "I came to get you."

She sat up slowly, pushing tangled locks of hair from her eyes. "Okay—why?"

His next words she could have predicted down to the letter. "We're leaving."

"I JUST DON'T UNDERSTAND." She raced along behind him, watching as he single-handedly destroyed the orderly precision of her new room. Clothes went flying, drawers hung askew. To a casual observer, it would look very much like she'd been robbed. "Why are we leaving? Dylan, we just got here. You were just crowned. There's still so much to do—"

"There's nothing left to do," he interrupted smoothly. Throughout the entire process he'd kept a wary eye on the window, tracking the quick progression of the sun. "We came here and got what we needed: control of Belaria's army. Now we need to get on to Rorque."

"*Rorque*?!" It actually took a second for Katerina's mind to switch tracks. For her to downscale so drastically from the length of a kingdom to a tiny rebel camp. "Why the heck would we go to Rorque now? We have *Belaria*, Dylan! The Northern Kingdom! We don't need to visit one camp."

"*One* camp?" He spun around so suddenly, she almost ran right into him. "Those camps are the backbone of this entire revolution. Those camps represent the people—not just the interests of one man. So, yeah, we're going to get that *one* camp on board. Just like we said we would."

Several problems with this logic. She didn't even know where to start. "Okay... but is it so bad when the interests of one man happen to be yours?" The look on his face silenced her, and she tried a different tack. "I get why you want to get Rorque on board, along with the rest of the camps but, Dylan—do you have to go *yourself*? I know you didn't like to hear it, but that officer did have a point about you being the king. Trying to keep you safe—"

"And what makes me so much better than that soldier with the blade?" he demanded. "The one who couldn't manage to stand up straight? The one who's going to march off and die just because *I've* decided it's the right thing to do?"

Here it was. The guilt. She'd been expecting it.

Growing up in the castle, she'd seen it many times. Falling on the heads of different kinds of men, in different stages of life.

Some of them ignored the feeling completely. Rationalized it away under the guise of 'divine right.' The fates had ordained them to rule these people, thus, anything they deemed prudent over the course of said rule was clearly meant to be.

Others felt it more deeply. Tortured every day by the sharp sting. This usually happened to men without royal blood. Men who'd been promoted, not ordained. Men who'd trained with the soldiers, fought with the soldiers, then suddenly had to send those same soldiers out to die.

Dylan's blood was as royal as it came, but she could have guessed that he'd be in the second camp. Amongst those who refused to avoid the responsibility. Refused to put others in harm's way based upon nothing but their own beliefs.

It wasn't the same when they were at Pora. Petra was in control there. She was the one giving the orders, making the final decisions. It was the same way with all the rebel camps. People volunteering to join the cause because they believed in it was one thing. Him giving a blanket order for them to do so was quite another.

She suddenly understood why he wanted to go to the camp himself. Why he didn't want to risk anyone else making the journey. They were going to be risking enough.

That being said, that's not exactly how the whole 'king' thing works.

"What makes me so much better?" Dylan demanded again. There was a hint of desperation in his voice, a desperation bordering on panic. Katerina bowed her head with a sigh.

"You're not better," she said quietly. "But you *are* the *king*."

He threw down the clothes he'd gathered in disgust. "Stop saying that like it's some kind of excuse! Stop saying that like it means something—"

"Stop pretending that it doesn't!" she countered, exasperated enough to fight back. "This whole time, I've been trying to give you space. Trying to give you support. Trying to understand that this whole thing has been a huge shock to you. You never planned on wearing the crown. This was never the future you envisioned." She crossed the room and stood right in front of him, matching him glare for glare. "But I never thought for a second that you didn't understand the weight of it, Dylan. The permanence. These people need a leader. And you took that crown. There's no going back now! There's no doing it halfway!"

His mouth opened to reply, but for once the man who had all the smart-ass answers had nothing to say. They stared at each other for a moment until he finally turned away, glancing out the window once more, jaw set firmly as he glared at the rising sun.

"I'm going to Rorque," he said shortly. "I'd like you to come with me. Since this whole thing was our idea, I feel it's the least we can do. If you'd like to stay back, where it's safe..."

He let the words trail off, making her feel like a monster with every second that passed.

On the one hand, he was absolutely right. What kind of message would it send if the queen herself wasn't willing to fight for her throne? On the other hand, he was absolutely wrong. What kind of uprising would it be if the very symbol of the revolution got herself killed before the battle?

Alwyn, forgive me, she said to herself, remembering her promise to the wizard to not do anything stupid. *You're really not going to like this...*

"Oh, give me that!" she snapped, yanking the knapsack out of his hands. "Of course I'm coming with you. And you didn't have to demolish my room," she added angrily, making her way back through and slamming drawers as she went. "You're all for standing up for the working class, but you don't seem to care that poor Anna's going to have to pick this all up when we leave..."

Together, they made a hasty pass through her chambers. Packing up anything they might need. Anything light enough for Katerina to carry around on her back. In the end, it wasn't much.

There were some sturdier travelling clothes—things meant for cold weather and hikes. A thick blanket, a pair of woolen gloves. But for the most part, the things Katerina needed weren't going to be found in a woman's room. Much less a lady of the court.

"I can't wear this dress," she murmured, looking down at herself in dismay. "I'd never make it through the underbrush."

The bag was packed, the room was fixed, and all that was left now was to prepare her person. Her luscious waves had already been yanked clear of her eyes with a simple leather cord, the rouge and lipstick had been scrubbed off her face, and those bracelets she'd found so charming the day before had been crammed roughly into her pack to sell or trade at a later date.

Dylan glanced over from where he was pacing impatiently in front of her bed.

"Not to mention, it doesn't have any belt loops. Where would you put your knife?"

Katerina froze a moment in surprise. The *exact* same question she'd been repeating to herself since catching her reflection in the mirror the day before. With a bit of effort, she shook it off. "Well, I'm not going to find any pants up here, and I doubt your room will have anything that would fit me. Where does that leave us?"

"The servants' hall," he answered automatically. "They should have things in your size. We can stop by on our way down to the armory to replenish our supplies."

Supplies.

Katerina hadn't thought in those logistical terms in what felt like quite a while.

"What about food?" she asked practically. "What about coin?"

Dylan opened his cloak to reveal a small leather pouch. "Plenty of coin. And Rorque is only two days' journey from here. Three, tops. We can get what we need from the forest."

Even as he said it, his entire face seemed to reanimate at the very thought. Walking on a bed of pine needles instead of the smooth ivory floors. Sleeping underneath the stars in his own clothes, instead of atop a pile of silk sheets, guarded by men whose names he would never know.

Katerina stared at him for a moment, wondering how many times in the next few days she was going to come to regret this decision.

"What about the others," she asked finally. "Are they waiting for us? Are they angry?"

There was a hitch in Dylan's pacing, followed by a deliberately casual voice. "They aren't...*angry*, per se. Aidan's orders were to go to Rorque anyway... so, he was fine with it."

The princess shot him a shrewd stare. "And the others? Rose, Tanya, Cass?"

"Rose is waiting downstairs," Dylan said quickly. "All ready to go."

There was a guilty pause.

"...and Tanya? Cass?"

Another pause. Even guiltier than the first.

"Well, since I already woke Rose and Aidan—and since Aidan's a vampire, that can be a risky move—I figured you could tell Cass and Tanya," he said lightly.

Katerina folded her arms across her chest with a disbelieving smile. "Oh, you did, did you?" she repeated acidly. "You thought *I* could tell them."

"...or I could do it."

"Now you're talking." She'd find a way to release the dragon in her again if she had to.

That thought nagged at her for a moment. She should be learning her ability. Secretly, so no one would know she didn't know how to shift properly. And somehow figure out how to master it. She needed to learn. Yet somehow there didn't seem to be any time. Guilt pulled at her insides. She needed to make time. Except, right now, Dylan was more important. She pushed the worry to the back of her mind. Dylan needed her.

CONSIDERING THAT KATERINA waited out in the hall while Dylan ventured fearfully forth into Cassiel and Tanya's shared chamber, considering that the walls were thick and lavish and coated with a million sound-absorbing things, it was impressive how well she could still hear the shouting.

"—Bloody idiot!"

"Cass, just listen to me—"

"My friend's a bloody moron! All this time, I thought you were just eccentric—*but no*! It turns out there's actually something fundamentally wrong with your brain!"

"It makes sense, Cass, just calm down and think—"

"THIS IS ME CALM!" the fae yelled. "Dylan, how many years have I been trying to get you to come here, to do this? A bloody ETER-

NITY! So you FINALLY do the right thing, come home, take back what's yours, and now... what? You want to run off again and play ranger?!"

"If you'd just stop shouting—"

"IT DOESN'T WORK LIKE THAT!"

A scary quiet fell over the hall, until Tanya's voice ventured up for the first time.

"...are we taking the crown?"

Ten minutes later, the others joined Katerina out in the hall. Dylan was giving Cassiel a wide berth, Tanya was fuming about 'leaving all her riches behind,' and the princess was very wisely avoiding everyone else's gaze. They joined up with Aidan and Rose in the lower hallways and continued on down to the servants' wing to get clothes.

"Oh, good..." Tanya held up a pair of trousers like a martyr. "...we're back to beige."

"Look on the bright side." Katerina tried to coax a smile. "At least it's not a corset."

"I rather liked the corset," Rose interjected, stripping off her clothes to change without the slightest concern as to who was watching. "It made for some interesting foreplay..."

Tanya gagged, and Katerina turned away with a sigh.

A few minutes later they were heading back down the hall towards the armory, looking a great deal more like the people who'd walked into Belaria just a few days before. Worn, weathered clothing. Soft-padded shoes. Moving with an ingrained synchronicity that spoke to life in the woods, as opposed to life in the palace. All that was missing now were the weapons.

And they had certainly come to the right place.

"All right." Tanya gazed around at the high shelves, each one glistening with more life-ending metal than Katerina had ever seen. "This is starting to make up for my loss of title..."

It was a warrior's paradise.

Everything from spears to swords. From long bows to maces. From arrows tipped with silver to a long-handled instrument so frightful and baffling Katerina felt the urge to give it some space. Serrated daggers small enough that she could slip them into her boots. Curved scimitars to lash to her back. There was even a series of deadly chakrams—bladed rings of iron that one could throw like a boomerang and decapitate from a great distance.

Aidan ran his finger along one of them with a shiver. "I've never liked these."

"Why not?" Dylan looped two onto his belt with a boyish grin. "They're damn useful."

"They're damn effective," Aidan replied evenly. "And judging from your cushy upbringing, Your *Majesty*, I'd be willing to bet you weren't often on the receiving end."

Cassiel seemed to be having a similar reaction to the row of halberds. A double-sided ax that was a favorite of the royal guard. The bows seemed to please him, however. So did the knives.

"Wait a second," Dylan thought back, shooting Tanya an incredulous look, "what made you think you were going to get a title? You're not even *from* here."

The shape-shifter looked at him as though he was being very stupid. "Oh, please. Your most trusted advisor?" She rolled her eyes and continued adorning herself with tiny throwing stars. "How could they *not* give me a title?"

Dylan shot Cassiel an automatic look, but the fae still wasn't speaking to him. Given the fact that he was currently holding a barbed javelin, the king wisely kept his feelings to himself.

"So, are we good to go?" Rose asked briskly, securing a leather strap to the top of her leg—a strap lined with a series of tiny knives. "We're heading straight to Rorque, right?"

"Straight to Rorque." Dylan nodded. "I was debating whether or not we should take along horses, but to be honest they're not much good in terms of—"

"Your Majesty!"

The gang whipped around in surprise to see the head of the council standing frozen in the doorway. One hand was holding a folded batch of parchment, while the other was still half-raised from where he'd pushed open the door.

"I'm sorry," he apologized quickly, "I didn't mean to interrupt. I was actually just going to bring you one of the blades you were admiring the other day. Captain Banks said you'd expressed an interest in having one for yourself..." He trailed off suddenly, his eyes drifting over his king's clothes. The weapons he'd already armed himself with. The overflowing satchel fastened to his back. "Your Majesty, please tell me you're not..."

Dylan tensed dramatically, and he lowered his head with a sigh.

"It's just that you've been away for so long," he said quietly. "People were just starting to get used to seeing you around here again. Walking these halls..."

The others graciously looked away, while Dylan took a step forward. Looking apologetic, but firm at the same time. "It won't be forever, but I need to finish what I started. To unite the rest of the rebel camps and rally them to our cause. To give our men the best chance I possibly can before sending them off to fight."

The guilt. The councilman recognized it, too.

"I could send a platoon of men to do that for you," he offered softly, knowing all the while that it was no use. "We need you *here*, my king. There's no need for you to go yourself—"

He cut himself off. Dylan didn't even have to. His answer was written all over his face. In the end, the councilman could only sigh.

"You probably don't remember—"

"I know who you are," Dylan interrupted quietly. "You're Atticus Gail. The man who urged my family to leave when there was still time enough for it to matter. You tried to save their lives."

Katerina's eyes shot to the back of his head, widening in shock. She'd had no idea that he'd recognized the man who'd been trying to help them. Of the tragic tie that connected them.

The man froze in astonishment, then hung his head. "It wasn't enough. I said everything I could, but no one would listen—"

"It was more than enough." A profound sadness flashed in Dylan's eyes, but at the same time his voice was unexpectedly kind. "Which is why I want you to take care of things here in my stead."

Atticus lifted his head in confusion. "My lord?"

"Ever since I came back you've been the only one I could count on, the only one I could trust." Dylan's gaze shone with sincerity as it locked onto the man. "I've seen what's happened to the kingdom in my absence, and I've seen all those things you've done to keep it on course. There's no one in the world I'd rather have leading these people while I'm away."

The councilman bowed his head, a bit overwhelmed with the immense compliment. But when he looked up, he was worried and tense.

"As kind as those words are, the people would rather have you leading them," he urged gently. "They've been waiting a long time for your return." There was a pause. "We all have."

This time, it was Dylan who looked overwhelmed. His lips parted for a moment, but he could think of nothing to say. Nothing but the truth. And his sincere desire to do the right thing.

"You understand why I have to leave?" he asked quietly.

Atticus sighed. "I understand why you think you do. I understand why you think there's something owed, some debt your bloodline is required to pay. And although I disagree with every bone in my body, I will follow your wishes to the letter. The people will be left in good hands."

Dylan's eyes glowed with gratitude as he reached out and shook the man's hand. "Thank you, Atticus."

The others silently filed past, each nodding to the man in turn.

"Stay safe, Your Majesty." The man gripped his hand tightly before visibly forcing himself to let go. "Limited fires at night. Send scouts on ahead. And if you should get into any trouble—"

"Thanks," Dylan cut him off, his eyes dancing with amusement, "but I read the ranger's handbook."

The councilman hedged his bets. "I don't suppose you'd let me send along a small escort of guards?"

Dylan flashed him a grin.

"Goodbye, Atticus."

With that, the six friends left the kingdom of Belaria behind, walking single-file into the woods with the ivory pillars of the palace glowing against the horizon. It was a bittersweet farewell. Their stay had been brief but it had left an impression on each of them.

Bringing the outcast into the fold. Giving the princess the start of her army.

Turning the ranger into a king.

Instead of taking his usual position up in front, Dylan had lingered near the back with Katerina. As they began to descend the first mountain, he paused at the top to take a final look back at the city he'd once called home.

The sunrise danced across his face as a strange wistfulness settled in his bright eyes.

Katerina slipped her hand into his. "You'll come back here again soon... I promise."

He glanced down at her before returning his eyes to the city. "Sure." His fingers tightened in a quick squeeze, but despite the reassurance a knot of dread hardened in the pit of her stomach. She couldn't help but think he didn't quite mean the word.

She couldn't help but think: *He doesn't plan on coming back at all.*

THAT FIRST NIGHT'S campfire turned into a virtual comedy of errors.

Armed for the first time with a bottle of kerosene, Tanya found herself accidentally lighting a fire so large it spread up the side of nearby tree. Once the tree had been put out and the friends had resettled elsewhere to avoid the smoke, one of the down blankets they'd been gifted from the palace caught a stray spark and they ended up having to move again. By the time they actually settled down long enough to get started on dinner, the smell of the palace's prize cuts of bacon smoking over the coals attracted some unwanted visitors. Most of them were small enough to be scared off. But the last one of them happened to be—

"Is that a bear?!"

In the end, their overabundance of supplies ended up shooting them in the foot. They packed up and moved again—much farther this time—and settled down in the dark with no supper.

"I still maintain that the kerosene mishap could have happened to anyone," Tanya insisted defensively, nestling down against Cassiel's chest. Her bright eyes were the only thing sticking up past the blanket, darting this way and that, daring anyone to disagree.

Like clockwork, one of their number was unable to resist.

"It wouldn't have happened at all, if you hadn't been tracing your name in oil onto the trunk of that tree." Dylan shot her a scathing look. "Yeah, I saw that."

"I wanted to light it before we left in the morning, leave my mark and all that." Her eyes widened with innocence as Cassiel cursed behind her in the dark. "I would have put it out..."

"What about you, Rose?" Katerina asked with a smile. "You find a way to leave your mark in this little corner of the world?"

The shifter smiled sweetly, twirling her knife in the air above her as she looked up at the stars. "Oh, I left my mark on several people..."

The princess snorted, then turned to her left. "Aidan?"

"I left my mark on the livestock population..."

Tanya screwed up her nose in distaste. "Aren't vampires supposed to hate that? Drinking the blood of animals?"

He shot her a silky smile. "Are you volunteering?"

Cassiel's eyes flashed in the shadows, and the conversation quickly fell flat. After a few seconds of silence, the princess shifted around to Dylan instead. He was sitting up on the blanket beside her, staring blankly into the dark woods.

At first, she thought he was just keeping an eye out for the bear. But there was a strange tension to the way he was holding himself. An ever-deepening crease between his eyes.

"Hey," she poked him gently, "what's on your mind?"

He shook his head quickly, looking as though she'd pulled him out of a deep trance.

"I was just thinking about when we first walked into the city and got arrested by those guards," he murmured. "There's just one thing that troubles me."

Rose lifted her head with a sarcastic smile. "*One* thing?"

"The guard who first took us into custody—Braxton—it was something he said." Dylan's eyes clouded as he remembered. "He said he was expecting us."

A sudden silence fell over the camp as the friends stared at each other in the dark.

Kat sucked in a sharp breath. *And how, in the name of the five kingdoms, could he have been expecting that?*

Chapter 9

The hike through the forest the next day was oddly beautiful. Crystal springs of water bubbling out of the earth. An emerald canopy of trees, speckled with little dots of gold where drops of the sun leaked through. A slow-moving river, as cool as it was refreshing, that followed along beside their every step. Winding its way slowly down the mountain as they followed through the trees.

For the first time since they'd embarked upon their impossible task all those months ago, the gang was well-armed, well-fed, well-rested, and well-supplied. For the first time, they felt like a group of people on a mission. Not a bunch of half-starved teenagers flitting from town to town. For the first time they felt like they were walking towards something, not just running away.

One would think their minds would have rested a little easier. One would think there'd have been a lightness to their step. But it couldn't be farther from the truth. All that peace of mind had been shredded the second Dylan recounted those fateful words: *We've been expecting you.*

"Maybe a scout saw us as we came out of the forest," Rose suggested, trying desperately to stay optimistic. "Someone who recognized you from the past."

"Someone who saw us, but managed to keep out of sight?" Cassiel inquired doubtfully.

Dylan nodded stiffly. "He's right. We would have seen any scouts a long time before they saw us. The path was clear for miles. There wasn't a way they could have seen us coming."

Rose flashed him a swift look before turning back to the forest. "Maybe you're not as good as you think you are."

"What does it matter?" Tanya asked for the tenth time. "Braxton might have been a prick before, but he works for *you* now, Dylan. He's a soldier under your command. The second we get back to Belaria, you can just order him to explain exactly what he meant." When no one answered, she turned to the princess in frustration. "Kat, back me up on this."

Katerina lifted her head, shaking off her own thoughts. "Hmm?"

Tanya flipped back her hair in frustration. "I said, what do you think?"

There was a pause.

"...about what?"

"Forget it." The shape-shifter waved her off. "You're useless."

Without a moment's pause, the discussion picked up right where it left off. Balancing tempers on the edge of a wire. Stretching nerves as far as they could go as burning speculation and dreadful predictions flew around in an endless loop.

The princess didn't hear it. She hadn't been paying attention for the last ten miles. The others might have been held up on the mystery, but she was focused on a mystery of her own.

Sure.

One little word, but it filled her with insurmountable dread. No matter what she did, she couldn't seem to get past the look on Dylan's face as he said it. That closed-off resignation as he took one last look towards Belaria. It was like he'd just shut down. Like whatever charisma that had propelled him forward thus far had simply turned off. Leaving him bereft in its wake.

Bereft and relieved.

As her eyes flickered across the sunlit canopy to where Dylan was leading them carefully up the path, she couldn't help but think...

He doesn't want to go home.

"This is a good place to stop," Dylan called suddenly, gesturing down the steep bank to the riverside. "We can get some food, then put in a few more hours before settling in for the night."

The others followed his lead without question, sliding gracefully down the slick grass until their boots slammed to a stop on the smooth pebbles that lined the shore. A pile of driftwood was quickly assembled to heat up a late lunch. The canteens were already being refilled with water.

Katerina watched them working from up amongst the trees, fiddling absentmindedly with the tip of her long braid. Normally, she'd be right down there with the others, pulling out supplies or setting up the caldron to cook, but today she was lost to the world. Playing it back, over and over in her mind. The one cursed word that had burrowed like a thorn into her side.

Sure.

"You okay?"

She jumped with a start, to see Dylan standing right in front of her. The man moved so quietly she hadn't even heard him approach. His dark hair spilled into his eyes as he stared at her with a curious expression, one that didn't entirely hide his concern.

She didn't bother to hide her true question. She jumped right in.

"Did you like that bedspread back at the palace?"

Okay... maybe she didn't jump *right* in.

He blinked.

"The bedspread?"

"Yeah," she nodded quickly, "the one in your room. Did you like it? Or do you think maybe you'll change it when you get back? The whole thing was a little dark for my tastes but, then again, I'm not the one who—"

"Kat," he was definitely smiling now, staring like she'd lost her mind, "what the heck are you going on about?"

She stared up at him for a frantic moment, then tried another tack. No matter what, she had to avoid looking at those dimples. They would only derail her. "What about the stables?"

He folded his arms across his chest, grinning ear to ear. "Okay, crazy, I'll play along. What about them?"

She ignored the crazy reference. Perhaps worried it was striking a bit too close to home.

"Dylan, they're far too small!" she exclaimed. "Anyone can see that they'll need to be expanded! So, are you planning on doing that yourself? Or delegating to someone else?"

"Did you get into those berries again?"

"There are bridges that need fortification. Schools that need funding." Her voice rose in panic as she prattled on. "Pieces of legislation that have been backed up for years—"

"Okay, seriously," he caught her by the shoulders, "what the heck is going—"

"Why aren't you planning on going back?!"

The words rang out between them, followed by a hushed silence that fell over the trees. The others stopped what they were doing and cast worried glances up towards the pair. Cassiel looked right about to join them, when Tanya caught him by the arm and held him back.

"Why aren't you planning on going back?" she asked again, feeling as though she'd been shaken to the core. "I know you're not. And the people *need* you. They *need* their king."

There was a chilling pause. One that seemed to stretch on for years.

"Why would you... I don't..." Dylan stammered a moment before falling quiet. A scary sort of quiet. One that told her she was right. "This isn't the place."

He started to walk away but she leapt forward and grabbed his sleeve, holding on with all her might. "Oh, no you don't! This is *exactly* the place—don't you dare walk away from me!"

His face paled about seven shades, but he held his ground. Eyes wide and defensive. Hyper-aware of the other people listening in. He tried to lower his voice, for all the good that would do.

"We got what we needed from Belaria—the army. The men will march when the time comes, and after they do I see no reason for me to go back and take up the crown."

There was a muted profanity from the river and Katerina's mouth fell open in shock. "No reason except that you *already did it*, Dylan!" she cried. "You made these people a promise; you can't go back on your word now!"

"The people were never supposed to know!" he shouted back, finally losing his temper. "I mean... of course they would eventually, but..." He took a step back, unaware of the subtle shudder that ran through his shoulders. "It was never supposed to happen the way it did. With everyone showing up just hours after it had happened. The entire thing got so far out of hand."

Katerina closed the distance between them, her voice both chilling and soft. "Out of hand?" she repeated, raising an eyebrow dangerously. "Dylan, you knelt in front of the altar. You took the orb and scepter. I put a *crown* on your head."

"You saw how it was there, Katerina!" he cried. "The bowing, and the scraping, and the scores of countless strangers who refuse to say your name! You saw the *bloody carpet*!"

The others shot each other confused looks but said nothing.

"So, tear out the carpet!" she shouted, throwing up her hands. "Loosen the protocol, make whatever changes you need. But you *cannot* just walk away from this! It's what you were born to do!"

"That's bull!" he countered. "We choose our own stars, princess! I don't have to die in that palace, just because I happened to be born there." His eyes glowed with a desperate sort of determination, willing the words to be true. "The second this fight is over, I can relinquish the crown to Atticus and everything can go back to the way it should be. The way it was before."

There was a tiny pause.

"The way it was before?" the princess repeated incredulously. "Dylan, how can you—"

She would have said more. She would have said a *lot* more.

But he silenced her with a simple question.

"Kat, why do you care?"

If he'd slapped her, it couldn't have felt any worse.

She reeled back in horror, eyes tearing up as she stared at him, numb with disbelief. She wanted to keep screaming. She was certainly screaming on the inside. But in the end all that came out was a quiet, trembling voice. "Do you see me in your future at all?"

A prince had to marry a princess. A queen had to marry a king. It was the rules by which the world lived. The basic structure that kept the kingdoms running.

He hadn't wanted it before; she'd known that. He'd wanted her, but not the lifestyle that came with her. The two of them could love as long as it lasted, right up to the gates of the palace, but that was where the fairytale would end. He'd made that quite clear.

But then... he'd changed his mind.

He'd gone back to Belaria. He'd pledged himself to his kingdom, acknowledged the legacy of his blood, accepted their crown. He'd been made king. He'd changed his mind.

...or so she'd thought.

Do you see me in your future at all?

Her question was still ringing through the forest. Every second it went unanswered the air between them seemed to thicken. The distance between them grew bigger and bigger.

Dylan was speechless. Absolutely, utterly speechless. Staring like he was seeing her for the first time. Several minutes went by, but still he was unable to answer.

It was an answer all by itself.

"Right." Katerina nodded swiftly, trying to keep her buckling legs straight. "Apparently not."

Suddenly, she wished she'd listened to him in the beginning. He was right; this wasn't the place. Four pairs of sympathetic eyes followed her every move, and all she wanted was to disappear.

No backing out now. Might as well finish what you started.

...since Dylan most certainly finished it himself.

"In that case, do whatever you want." She looked quickly to the side to wipe her eyes before turning back to the ranger. She refused to think of him as a king. "The second the battle is over, the two of us can go our separate ways. And I see no need to make that harder in the meantime. You can rest assured you won't be leaving anything behind. Whatever there was between us... is over."

Chapter 10

Never break up with someone mid-road-trip. It's exactly as awkward as it sounds.

Neither Katerina nor Dylan said anything for the rest of the day. Not a single word. He looked over at her several times. He looked as though he'd been pierced with a silver blade. But he never tried to speak. Never tried to get her to speak either. And she kept her eyes forward.

The others tried bravely to fill in the space, forcing questions and awkward spills of conversation. But after a few fruitless tries they gave up, and the little consortium continued in silence. Following the winding river. Trying very hard to act as though the entire thing had never happened. Only Tanya fell back in an unexpected show of support. Linking her arm through the princess' without ever saying a word.

The sun hung stubbornly in the sky, refusing to fall and lessen Katerina's pain, and it felt like ages later before they finally came to a fork in the road. Tinged with golden shadows at dusk.

It was here that they stopped.

"Which way?" Rose asked, the first one to speak in hours.

Rather than looking at Dylan to answer the question, Katerina turned to Cassiel. The fae was just as good a guide. There was no reason for direct contact when such a perfect intermediary stood between them. Cassiel wasn't looking at the ranger, either; he was frowning at the river instead.

Tensing automatically, she followed his gaze.

Has it always been that strong?

Somehow, over the course of the last few hours, what had started out as a peaceful little stream had suddenly escalated into a raging tide. Torrents of frothy white rapids pushed violently past each other, swelling the banks of the river, splashing up over the sides. She could no longer gauge the depth, nor did she have any delusions that she could survive a swim to the other side.

None of that would have been a problem if one of the paths hadn't been a bridge. A bridge that was now partially submerged in the raging water.

"Do you think it's the wizard again?" Tanya asked quietly, cringing back a step as yet another plank of wood vanished under the crushing tide. "Up to his old tricks?"

Rose shot them a quick look, but Cassiel kept his eyes on the water. The very ground they stood on trembled with its vibrations. Vibrations that were shaking the posts of the bridge.

"Yes and no. This is from the snow melt—more specifically, the avalanche." He crossed his arms over his chest, looking deeply uncomfortable. "He most certainly caused that, but this? This could just be the fallout. Nothing sinister."

"Nothing sinister," Aidan repeated under his breath. "Just the fallout from an avalanche brought forth by a dark wizard out for blood."

Cassiel shot him a dry look. "Yes. That."

"So, what are we going to do?" Katerina asked with a touch of impatience. Ever since Dylan's and her little chat, she was more than eager for this journey to be over. Truth be told, she had no idea if the gang would even remain together after the alliance with the camps had been made. Odds were, Aidan would go back to Pora, and the rest of them would go their separate ways. "Can we cross it? I'm taking it that Rorque is on the other side."

Cassiel nodded slowly, then shot a reflexive glance at Dylan. The ranger was staring at the river in stony silence. Unwilling to weigh in either way.

"It *is* the fastest way to Rorque, but..." He glanced again at Dylan, then sighed in frustration when the ranger didn't meet his gaze. "A little help here? What do you want to do?"

Slowly, Dylan raised his eyes. There wasn't a shred of emotion on his face. He was simply blank. The same way he'd been when he looked back at Belaria for the last time.

"We can't cross," he said quietly. "And I'm not convinced it isn't the wizard. I'd be willing to bet that if we went back the way we came, the water would be just as high."

"But, why?" Rose asked quickly, staring around as though the man might be lurking in the bushes, watching his little scheme play out. "Why wouldn't he want us to take the bridge?"

Dylan glanced at the opposite path and sighed, running a tired hand back through his hair. "Because we can't go that way, either. It's a dead end."

Cassiel shot him a quick look, but let it go. Katerina wasn't so generous.

"What?" she demanded, looking at the fae instead of the ranger. "What aren't you saying?"

The fae froze in the sudden spotlight, caught in a place he didn't want to be. His eyes flitted Dylan's way again before giving up and answering the question himself.

"It's not a dead end, per se. It's just... that path takes us directly through the Kingdom of Carpathia. Straight through the heart of their lands."

Carpathia.

The name had some sinister undertones but failed to ring a bell.

"And that would be a bad thing?" Katerina asked sharply.

The fae shifted on his feet, looking more and more uncomfortable.

"The Carpathian queen is everything they say. Cruel, cunning. With a taste for bloodshed and a knack for making people disappear. A perfect match for her people. She's been their unchallenged ruler for as long as I can remember. There's a chance she may be older than me."

"Older than you?" Katerina repeated in surprise. "How is that possible?"

"Some say she's part vampire," Tanya answered, with an involuntary look towards Aidan.

"She's not," Dylan answered automatically. Then he amended, "She might be."

"The point is, we may have been able to deal with the queen." Cassiel's eyes darted once more to the ranger. "But she and Dylan... have a history."

Katerina's spine stiffened as she turned slowly to look at him.

Why am I not surprised?

"It was a long time ago," Dylan said swiftly. "There's a chance she doesn't even remember."

Cassiel shot him a dubious look, which he was determined to ignore.

"A long time ago?" Rose asked with a mixture of a grin and a frown. "How long?"

"Like, two years."

Katerina closed her eyes and turned away, while the shifter burst out laughing.

"Two years?! So you were about sixteen years old when you were playing around in the bed of the infamous Carpathian queen?" She laughed again. "I have to say, Hale, I'm impressed."

"Don't be impressed," Dylan muttered. "It didn't end well."

Cassiel pursed his lips, trying to look on the bright side. "It didn't end *that* badly."

"She set my hair on fire."

"Yes, aside from that."

"Who cares?" Katerina interjected suddenly, drawing everyone's gaze. "Dylan's right. It was a *long* time ago. And if we avoided every kingdom where he screwed some random woman, we'd never make it home." The ranger flinched, but she continued. "At any rate, we can move fast, speak to no one, and keep to the shadows. There's a chance the queen will never know we're there."

The girls nodded, Dylan stared down at his shoes and Cassiel shook his head, the hint of a frown on his face. It looked as though he was going to press for the river instead, but before he could open his mouth to speak there was a sudden snapping sound as the ropes holding the bridge gave way.

With a weary sigh, Cass turned towards the other path. But not without a dire warning. "She'll know we're there," he said with grim certainty. "I'm afraid she's not going to be thrilled to see us..."

Chapter 11

They say that over time people start to resemble their pets. Well, Katerina was convinced that in the decades of the queen's twisted rule the very land of Carpathia had grown in accordance.

The forested mountains that had preceded it were so lovely that when they passed over the border into Carpathian lands, it came as a visceral shock. Gone was the green. Gone were the trees and the water and the mountains. The land in front of her was cracked, and dry, and impossibly flat—alternating different colors of grey and burnt red, like some long-abandoned chess board.

Spires of jagged obsidian stretched up in random outcroppings, reaching towards the dusky sky like withered fingers clawing their way from the ground. Large, domed buildings had been built into the very foundations. A hive of insects clinging to the side of each rock. There was no way to differentiate one from another. No personal touches or signs of life that would give them away. The overwhelming theme of Carpathia seemed to be desolation and survival. A brutal land that had bred a brutal people, led by an even more brutal queen.

Katerina heard a sharp crackling and glanced down in horror to see that she'd accidentally stepped on the bleached skeleton of what might have been a cat. Her mouth opened in a silent gasp, but Tanya quickly pulled her forward as the gang kept moving.

Sticking to the shadows. Sticking *close* together. Ignoring the sudden chill that swept over their skin and the way that the hair on the back of their necks was standing on end. Ignoring how, with every inch the sun slipped below the horizon, more and more people flooded the streets.

Ignoring the way they were suddenly no longer alone.

"Oh, pardon me!"

The hulking shape of a man suddenly stumbled into their path, straightening up with a grin that mocked his manners and convinced Katerina it was very much intentional. He was just as tall as the men she was travelling with, maybe even a little more, with thick bands of muscles stretched beneath a worn coat and a row of yellowing teeth, as chipped and jagged as the obsidian that scarred the barren landscape.

"I don't believe I've seen you here before. You must be new." He looked them up and down with a lascivious smile; it didn't seem to much matter if he was looking at the women or the men. "What a treat. It isn't often that we get visitors..."

Katerina's heart leapt into her throat, and she inched subconsciously closer to the others. It helped a great deal that they were armed, head to toe, with brand new weapons from the palace. On the other hand, she couldn't help but fear that it made them even more of a target. These people seemed the type to embrace that kind of challenge. Already, more were on their way.

"Rudo, don't be a fool." One hulk was replaced with another, pushing the first roughly to the side as he bore down upon the friends with the same leering smile. "These people aren't visitors, they're our guests."

Something about the way he said *guests* made the princess break out in a cold sweat. For one of the first times since it had happened, she was suddenly reminded of the two soldiers who had lured her into the woods—the day she'd first discovered that Dylan was a wolf. They looked very different from these men here, but there was something similar in their eyes. That same predatory hunger that made her feel vulnerable and small.

"We're just passing through," Dylan said in a carefully measured voice, loud enough to be heard but soft enough not to escalate matters further. "Travelling on the King's Road."

It may not have been confrontational, but at the same time a subtle threat hung in his words. Those travelling on the royal road were granted the protection of the crown. To attack such a traveler became a royal offense—one most people weren't willing to risk.

Then again, Katerina wasn't sure those rules mattered in a place like this. If anything, it made the man smile even wider.

"Are you, now?" His eyes were black as coal and raked across Dylan with frightful efficiency, missing not a single detail. From the way he was dressed, to the way he was armed, to the casual tension in his position. A man who was always poised to strike. "And where might you be headed, little traveler? And with such beautiful friends."

Three more men had appeared behind him. None of them registered the others, but all of them seemed to have the same thing on their minds. At the very least, they were looking for a fight.

If they could get something more than that...

"We're headed to the Dunes."

Cassiel stepped suddenly forward, blocking the women as he came to Dylan's side. He had pulled a scimitar from the sheath on his back and was casually stroking a finger along the curved blade. The sight of it stopped the men in their tracks. The Fae were not to be taken lightly. Nor were they known for their even tempers. They were also thrown by his mention of the Dunes.

"The Dunes?" the man named Rudo repeated, sharing a swift look with the others. "Why in seven hells are people like you going to the Dunes?"

The Dunes were on the far outer rim of the five kingdoms. In the place that most people simply referred to as the Badlands, when they were forced to refer to it at all. It was the place where Kailas had gotten his hellhounds. A realm of ash and death and dust. A place so evil and corrupt it made Carpathia itself look like a child's playground.

"This one's uncle is heading up a faction there." Cassiel jerked his head first to Dylan before gesturing to the three women standing just behind. "He asked that we bring him a gift from the five kingdoms upon our return. I like to think we've found a nice selection."

There was a wicked snickering throughout the men as their eyes found the spaces between the ranger and the fae and came to rest on the women. For the first time, Rose looked like she wished she was wearing more clothing. Katerina was openly shaking, and Tanya's grip tightened on the handle of her blade.

"You arm them?" Rudo asked curiously, tilting his head to the side with that same hungry gleam. "Why?"

"My uncle likes a bit of a challenge," Dylan answered coldly. "He's not in the habit of waiting, and I'm not in the habit of explaining myself. Like I said, we're just passing through."

This time it was easy to hear the threat in the words. But this time that threat hit home.

The men parted before him, like the waves of an intemperate sea. Together, and with the greatest possible haste, the six friends stepped through the gap, hurrying up the road as score upon score of townsfolk came out to see them.

Maybe we can pass through unnoticed. Maybe the queen will never know we were there. Katerina kept her eyes locked on the ground, keeping right in step with Aidan. *I'm an idiot.*

No one else made to stop them, and they faced no more obstacles as they made their way across the wasteland. Little torches dotted the shadowy landscape, reflecting crimson flames in the eyes of the people following their every move. But for the most part, the land was quiet. The sky was black and devoid of stars. Nothing but flocks of screeching crows circling overhead.

Not since they'd been trapped in the endless forest of Laurelwood had Katerina felt such visceral terror, and despite the deadly curse she still might have traded the shadowy darkness for a few minutes in those sunlit trees.

She felt a stab of belated terror as she imagined a sixteen-year-old Dylan wandering through these lands on his own. Those blue eyes wide with silent fear. A circle of crows screaming overhead.

"Cass," she whispered, pulling gently on his sleeve.

The fae glanced around before falling back a step, keeping a careful eye on their surroundings and Tanya at the same time.

"What you said about the Carpathian queen," she began uncertainly. "About her and Dylan having a rough history..."

Strangely enough, it wasn't the sex that bothered her. It wasn't the fact that, for whatever reason, a teenage Dylan had found himself ending up in the royal bed. It was the queen herself. It was what Katerina was terrified she might be capable of.

"Kat, I don't know all the specifics," Cassiel answered quietly, "but I would imagine that very little of it was his choice—"

"No, it's not that," she said quickly, cringing into the safety of his arm as they passed another bonfire. "I'm worried about her finding him. Wouldn't it be safer for him to shift?"

There was a slight hitch in Dylan's step. It was impossible to keep anything from the ears of a shifter. And Cassiel softened just the slightest degree.

"Under most circumstances, yes. But there are no animals here. He wouldn't last long."

"Why are there no..." she started to ask, then forced herself to stop. Whatever it was, she didn't think she wanted to hear the answer.

So it was that they continued in silence, gradually leaving the inhabitants of the first outpost behind. The moment they did, they drastically quickened their pace. Retreating in dignity only for as long as was necessary before breaking into a run.

Katerina still didn't have the natural endurance of the others. She might have technically joined their shifter ranks, but she was new to the powers in her blood. Unable to summon them up when she needed. Still trapped under the limited guise of humanity.

Her breath came in short, quick bursts as she carried on for as long as she could. Struggling to keep pace. Struggling to keep silent. She about had a heart attack when the ground beneath her suddenly disappeared as Aidan lifted her up into his arms.

"It's okay," she flushed bright with shame, "you don't have to..."

But she trailed off, unable to finish the sentence. It was a lie anyway. If he hadn't acted when he did, she doubted she could have lasted even another mile.

Instead, she clung to him breathlessly. Wrapping her arms around his neck and burying her face in his chest to hide her eyes from the nightmare creatures all around her. Dylan glanced back only for a fleeting moment, then quickened his pace. Saying not a word.

On and on they went, spanning countless miles, though there were countless more to go. It seemed a foregone conclusion that they would not be setting up camp for the night. They would not be stopping anywhere in this god-forsaken country but would continue on until they were through.

Aidan's pace never faltered, and his arms never tired. It seemed as though all the stories of the infallible strength of vampires were true. The wind whipped through his dark hair as he pulled in steady, shallow breaths. Calming Katerina's own as they fell into a steady rhythm.

"Thank you," she whispered, so softly she was confident only he could hear.

He glanced down in surprise before looking back up with a faint smile. "I thought you'd fallen asleep."

"Sleep? Here?" She stifled a shudder. "Not likely."

She felt the soft shaking of laughter in his chest. He alone seemed much more at ease in the land of shadows than the rest. Not that he was enjoying himself—far from. But it didn't seem to affect him the way it did the others. It didn't seem to crawl under his skin.

"So, I'm guessing this isn't exactly what you signed up for," she teased, casting a tentative glance into those luminous eyes. "When the six of us left Pora?"

"Are you kidding?" His lips quirked up with a grin. "Saving damsels, dodging Carpathian thugs... it's all part of the job. At any rate, it's hardly a strain on my time. If I was back at Pora, all I'd be doing is watching Segor the troll beat Ralfgnar the giant in an ill-advised wrestling match. *Again*."

She shook her head incredulously, gazing up at him with a smile. "I don't get it. How can you be so calm?"

The question seemed to surprise him, and he looked down with a smile of his own. "What's the alternative?"

She was about to answer, when the entire party screeched to a sudden halt. Aidan dropped her immediately and pushed her back out of sight, but not before she glimpsed the thirty or more Carpathian soldiers standing in their way. Spears at the ready. Lips pulled back in garish grins.

One man stepped forward. A man who would give the late magistrate a run for his money.

"We heard there were six travelers passing through." His eyes sparked with torchlight as he looked each of them over in turn. "On their way to the Badlands."

How the heck did he hear that so fast?!

As if to answer her question a crow screeched loudly overhead, and Katerina stifled a shiver.

"Good news travels fast."

Dylan and Cassiel shared a quick look, but neither of them said a word more. Katerina got the terrible impression that they were out of moves to play in this particular hand. The man stepped even closer. He seemed to be thinking the same thing.

"Well, far be it from me to delay your travels, but the queen would like a word."

Just like that, any delusions of safe passage vanished in the blink of an eye.

Just like that, the six friends wished they had taken their chances with the bloody bridge.

KATERINA HAD TROUBLE seeing much of anything after that. With a thirty-man escort, the six friends were forcibly removed from the King's Road and taken instead down the splintering shale path that led to the palace. Under most circumstances, she would have bet on her five friends out-maneuvering a thirty-man company any day. But these weren't most circumstances. And the guards serving as their escort could hardly be described as men.

They were massive. Each one built like an ox, and armed with a series of grisly, spikey-looking weapons Katerina had never seen, but knew instinctively she'd never be able to forget. But they weren't massive in the same way as giants or trolls. There was nothing lumbering or slow-witted about them. Each one moved with a speed and stealth that defied their size and left the princess scrambling to keep up with their pace.

They were the type of 'men' that her brave friends refused to even engage. Not because they were certain they wouldn't win, but because they were certain they wouldn't win without massive casualties on their own side. Because the second they took one down (if that was even possible), two more would rise up to take their place. Because it was futile. Dangerous and futile to resist.

They had, however, confined the girls to the middle. That's why Katerina was having such a hard time trying to see. The second the company had stepped forward the three men had closed ranks—wedging the girls into a tight space between them. There was barely room to walk. There was barely room to breathe. But as Katerina glimpsed flashes of the long-toothed smiles bearing down on her from either side, she had to admit she was intensely relieved that there was at least one body between her and the Carpathians.

For the next hour, at least, they walked on a straight path leading directly back the way they'd come. Katerina tried to look for anything she might recognize but the world was dark, and it was hard enough to keep pace let alone see over the tall shoulders that surrounded her. In the end, she simply kept her eyes on the ground and tried to stay standing. Measuring each uneven step before lowering her boot. Swaying slightly as the long hours since departing Belaria began to take their toll. Terrified of what might happen if she was to disrupt the rhythm and fall.

Aidan was right. I should have tried to get some sleep.

Then, just as suddenly as they'd left the torch-lit trail behind, Katerina found herself walking on smooth stone. It was the same obsidian as she'd seen in the first township, just as sharp, and smooth as glass. The pathway narrowed, forcing them to cluster closer together before they finally passed under a pointed arch and Katerina found herself suddenly inside the Carpathian palace.

Her first thought was that it was freezing.

The entire place seemed to be carved out of the same black stone. There was no cloth or fabric of any kind. No windows. Just jagged openings cut into the rock, designed to look like spades. Nothing to keep the frigid night from rushing in, and nothing to heat the air already inside.

Her next thought was that it was dark.

She couldn't remember ever seeing a place so dreary. It would have been bad enough in the daytime, but without the rays of the sun there was nothing present to light their way. She kept waiting for her eyes to adjust. For them to get to some sort of antechamber—the kind with torches and tapers. But that never happened.

The Carpathian troops didn't mind. Their eyes seemed to have adjusted to scampering around in the dark, like termites returning to the hive. But the darkness was a hindrance to her.

On more than one occasion, she found herself reaching out to Tanya for balance. When the group made a sharp turn and came to a sudden stop, she slipped completely and fell to the ground.

It was exactly as she'd feared. The second she broke ranks, provided even a sliver of an opening, the Carpathian horde swarmed in to take advantage.

Oh, crap!

There was a shuffling of bodies, followed by the clash of metal, followed by a loud hiss. It was the hiss that threw her, and she looked up to see Aidan angled defensively over her body, his fangs bared, his bright eyes flashing pure murder in the dark.

The Carpathians didn't step back but made no move to get closer. They merely tightened their grip upon both Dylan and Cassiel—both of whom they'd seized the second they tried to help.

The vampire was a different story, but he was drastically outnumbered. Already, the princess could hear their soft laughter as they circled around behind him in the dark. Tanya and Rose whipped around to face them, reaching swiftly for their blades, when a cool hand flashed out of nowhere and pulled Katerina back up to her feet.

She felt the muscles in Aidan's shoulders tense as he pulled her tight to his side. Saw a shiver of anticipation twitch through his fingers as they curled into claws. Dylan tried to shout something, but a heavy hand was clamped over his mouth. The vampire tilted his head to the side but never lost focus. His gaze was fixed on the men standing in front of him. His body was curled and ready to fight. The first soldier was in striking distance, the second was close behind. His eyes were already on the third, playing out the fight seven moves in advance.

His grip on Katerina tightened. A low growl started rumbling in his chest—

"I can see the party started without me."

The Carpathians leapt back like they'd been burned, releasing the prisoners at once and blushing like little schoolboys as a tall figure swept out of the shadows. Katerina sucked in a silent breath, trying to look past Aidan's shoulders, but she was unable to see in anything but silhouette until a pair of torches blazed to light, illuminating the woman standing in their midst.

The princess' eyes widened as her mouth fell open in surprise. There wasn't a doubt in her mind as to who the woman was. There wasn't a doubt in her mind as to what the woman could do.

THIS is the queen of Carpathia?

For once, the legends didn't disappoint.

She was shockingly beautiful. With ice-green eyes, blood-red lips, and tumbling waves of onyx hair, she was one of the most beautiful women Katerina had ever laid eyes on. But beneath the beauty was something dangerous. Something cold.

Her features were delicate, but hard. Her ivory skin as smooth as glass, and sharp as the rocks they were standing on. It was impossible to tell her age. It was impossible to tell anything about her, save for that which she wanted you to see.

"Boys, what did I tell you? I wanted you to bring them back alive."

There was no warmth beneath the smile. No light dancing in her eyes. It was as if someone had reanimated the world's loveliest corpse. Filling her with a dark and vengeful spirit. One that seemed to radiate around her, haunting her every step.

The Carpathian guard who'd captured them out on the road, the one who'd coincidentally been standing closest to Aidan, fell at once to his knees.

"My apologies," he panted. "We were just bringing them in to see you—"

"*No*," she corrected with that same lifeless smile, "you were just getting ready to rip them to pieces for a chance to get at that girl."

She held out her hand, delicate porcelain framed by five pointed nails, and gestured for him to get to his feet. Their eyes met for a fleeting moment before she continued towards the others, trailing a careless finger along the base of his neck.

For a second, Katerina thought that was the end of it. That the queen had called him out for disobedience and moved on. Then there was a soft gasping sound and the soldier in question fell to his knees once more. His throat sliced open. His blood spilling out onto the floor.

A second later, all was quiet. Save for the crimson drip coming from the queen's nails.

"I specifically wanted them alive."

The rest of the Carpathians cringed backwards, but the queen no longer had any time for them. Something else had caught her attention and she swept towards the group of friends, her red dress whispering over the stone.

She came to a stop in front of Dylan. They were exactly the same height.

"I don't believe it."

For the first time, her eyes showed a spark of life.

"Dylan Aires. It has been a long time."

THE REST OF THE GUARDS vanished. The rest of the torches were lit. And the six friends found themselves suddenly standing in a room alone with the queen. A queen who needed no guards to protect her. A queen who was looking positively delighted at who had stumbled into her palace, just as thrilled as Cassiel had warned she would be.

She approached slowly, like a spider savoring the sight of a fly caught in her web.

"An uncle in the Dunes?" Her eyes glittered as she lifted Dylan's chin with one pointed nail, a nail still dripping with the blood of her soldier. "That's curious, as I was under the impression all your family was dead."

Under most circumstances, he would have flushed. Today, he paled.

"The Carpathians are known to have a temper just as fiery as their queen," he answered softly. "I was just trying to avoid any complications—"

"You were just trying to avoid seeing me," she interrupted. Her voice cracked out like a whip, then melted into honeyed tones. "And that hurts, Dylan. That you would pass through without stopping in to say hello. Especially after your last visit." Her eyes glowed like fiery coals. "I remember the two of us having such a... tender time."

A shiver ran through his entire body, but he didn't surrender an inch. The queen grinned, pleased with her own little game, and moved slowly down the line.

"And what do we have here... a dual-eyed shifter. A *shape*-shifter, that's a little more interesting. A prince of the Fae—Dylan, he's just as pretty as you. The renegade Damaris princess. I have a feeling, my dear, that we'll be circling back to you... and a *vampire*!"

Katerina, still reeling from the fact that the queen had discovered all their secrets so easily, watched as she looked between Aidan and Dylan with obvious delight.

"A vampire, Dylan. You surprise me." Those onyx waves trembled as she clapped her hands. "I seem to remember you being less than tolerant of their kind."

"Only on occasion," Dylan answered stiffly. "When their kind gives in to their darker urges."

A silent look passed between him and the queen before she turned back to Aidan.

"Well, I'm most pleased to meet you," she said animatedly. Strangely enough, Katerina got the feeling she meant it. "Any vampire is most welcome within Carpathian lands."

Aidan had frozen still with shock. His eyes flickered once between the queen and Dylan before he inclined his head with a polite smile. "Thank you... milady."

"Oh, no need to stand on formalities." She tilted her head with a tinkling laugh, like glass raining down upon pavement. "You'll find we have very little of them here."

"Jazper," Dylan took a step forward, fixing the queen squarely in those piercing eyes, "what do you want?"

For a second, her smile faltered. Then it returned full-force. "Excuse me?"

A muscle twitched in the back of Dylan's jaw, but he kept his composure. "For safe passage. What do you want in exchange for letting all of us go?"

All of us. Katerina noticed the slight stress he put on the word. As if he was anxious to move on to the next step, while worried that some of their number might be left behind.

But the queen wasn't yet finished with her game.

"What is this?" she asked innocently, pretending to be surprised. "So many years, yet you're ready to leave so soon? The Dylan I knew was young, sweet, affectionate." The edges of her lips curled up in a wicked smile. "Inexperienced, but as I recall you were certainly willing to please—"

"*Enough!*" he interrupted, temper getting the better of him.

"Most of all," she raised her voice over his, "you were never one to shy away from a little bit of pain. No matter how it left its *mark*."

He flinched, as though he'd been hit. One hand drifting compulsively to his collar. He lowered it again slowly, staring deep into her eyes. "What do you want?"

The queen smiled again, but all the playfulness was gone. Nothing remained but a chilling expectation.

One that made Katerina instinctively frightened of whatever was to come.

"How about an encore performance?"

There was a second of silence. The entire room seemed to ache with it. Then the princess spoke without thinking, her words hissing through the air.

"Excuse me?!"

Dylan had frozen dead still. The queen smiled. Her eyes never left him, though Katerina got the feeling she was watching them both. Seeing more than she should. Reading between the lines.

"I would be happy to grant you safe passage through my kingdom," she repeated lightly, as if they were discussing where they ought to brunch. "If our new king will spend the night with me."

Absolutely not! Abso-freakin'-lutely not!

Katerina wanted to scream it at the top of her lungs. She didn't quite understand why the others weren't screaming the same thing. She didn't quite understand why Dylan was just standing there, staring at the evil woman with wide, haunted eyes.

The queen flashed a final smile and disappeared, vanishing into the shadows. "I'll give you a few moments to decide..."

Chapter 12

"**I** say we kill this bitch and get the heck out of here."

Katerina didn't mince words. Nor did she do anything to hide her anger. The second the queen was gone she rounded on the others, rallying them to her cause. In her mind, it should have been the easiest decision they'd ever made. In her mind, there wasn't even a question.

So why were the others just standing there, shifting uneasily on their feet?

"Well?" she demanded, well-aware that her voice was likely to carry down the cavernous stone hall. "Who's with me?"

In the tortured silence that followed, no one dared to speak. Then, with a look of profound devastation, Cassiel lowered his head with a sigh. "It's not that simple."

Katerina almost slapped him right then and there. What the heck was he thinking? He was supposed to be Dylan's BEST FRIEND! He should be the one leading the opposition—not her!

"Are you freakin' kidding me?"

Her own voice was soft and deadly to her ears.

"We can't just kill the queen of Carpathia," Rose said quietly, interceding on his behalf. "I know how you must feel, Kat, but try to think it through—"

"Coming from the girl who would have sex with anyone!" Katerina snapped. "And, actually—*yes*, we *can* kill the queen of Carpathia. *I* can." Her power was tied to her emotions, right? Well, she had never been so enraged. Already, little flickers of fire were rising from the tips of her fingers, just dying to be set free.

Aidan stared at her silently. Tanya looked like she might be sick.

"It's not that we can't *kill* her," Cassiel explained, making a monumental effort to say every word, "it's that we *can't* kill her. Dylan was just crowned king of Belaria. We're about to march on the High Kingdom. The last thing we need on our hands is a war with the Carpathians."

"It would divide our forces," Rose agreed softly. "Cost us men and supplies we desperately need—and that's only *if* the six of us end up making it out of here alive." A little tremble rattled through her shoulders as she lifted her eyes to the shadowy hall where the queen had disappeared. "She didn't seem like the type to take *no* for an answer..."

I can't believe it! I can't BELIEVE they're even considering this!

"Tanya!" The princess whirled around. "Help me out here!"

Something about the black floors, black walls, and black ceilings made the tiny girl seem even smaller. She was all hair and eyes, avoiding everyone's stare, trembling in the dark.

"...what if Kat shifted?"

"Yes!" Katerina threw up her hands in triumph, making a mental note to give her friend a medal of honor the second she got back the throne. "What if I shifted. Like, *right now*?"

"You shift now, and it's exactly the same as if you set the queen on fire." Cassiel shook his head, flexing his hand. Ever since the queen made her demand, he'd been gripping one of the daggers he'd taken from the palace with extraordinary strength. He didn't seem to realize his palm was bleeding. "You'll turn the kingdom against you, and then we'll be fighting a war on two fronts."

With every logical objection, Katerina found herself slipping further and further away. She felt Dylan slipping further and further away. It was like she'd already lost him.

"Okay, then, what if I didn't shift?" she said desperately. "What if we just escaped? I'm serious, Cass, we could jump out these windows right now. It might be a little risky, but—"

"*Katerina*," his voice was strained, "it's *exactly* the same thing. There's nothing we can do here to avoid angering the queen, except—"

He cut himself off suddenly, eyes flashing without permission to his friend. Dylan was still standing in a daze, exactly where the queen had left him. He'd yet to take a full breath.

"Dylan," the fae began softly, "if this isn't something..." He trailed off painfully, unsure how to proceed. One look at his friend's face and his own logic went out the window. "We could try to bargain with her. Offer her anything else—"

"There is nothing else," Dylan spoke for the first time. "She has everything she needs."

Katerina's jaw fell to the floor. Of all the people gathered, of every person standing in the room, she thought she could count on at least one. But that one person just sealed his own fate.

"You CAN'T be serious!"

Dylan's entire body seemed to sigh as he turned to face her. It was the first time the two of them had really looked at each other since their impromptu breakup by the river. The first time their eyes had met, and the sight of him was tearing Katerina apart.

"What do you want me to say—"

"I WANT YOU TO SAY NO!"

The words echoed in the monstrous hall, tearing straight through the heart of them with each pass. Somewhere in the darkness, the queen was laughing. Somewhere in the shadows, the guards were poised to kill. But Katerina didn't see any of them. She had eyes for only one man.

A man who was being ripped away from her, piece by piece.

"I want you to NOT sleep with this diabolical woman!" she cried, unable to stop the tears from streaming down her face. "I want to you to call her back here and say NO!"

"You think I WANT to sleep with her?" Dylan shouted back, eyes tightening as all those walls he'd worked so hard to build started crumbling before her very eyes. "You think the very thought of it isn't KILLING me just to—"

"Then DON'T do it!"

Deep down, Katerina knew that what the others had been saying made sense. Deep down, she understood she was being short-sighted and certain sacrifices had to be made. Very, *very* deep down, she was painfully aware that this was a lot harder on Dylan than it was on her.

But looking at him across the room... none of that mattered.

She might have broken up with him. She might have told him, just a few short hours ago, that whatever had been between them was over. That their fleeting, star-crossed romance had come to an end. But it was a lie. It was a lie, and they both knew it.

She was in *love* with him.

In a way that knew no limits. In a way that made her stupid and selfish. In a way that was as permanent as the stars in the sky. There was no *over* with them. There could never be an over. They belonged to each other. Body and soul.

And the thought of him giving that body to another woman...

"*Please.*" Her voice dropped to a sudden whisper as her entire body started shaking. "Please don't do it. Just tell her no."

A look of actual pain shot across Dylan's face. As though he'd been pierced with some invisible dagger. He took an involuntary step towards her, lifting his arms, then caught himself.

Breathing hard, he stayed exactly where he was. Hands clenched into fists. Jaw rigid and set.

"If I do that, there's a chance she'll kill you," he said shortly. "The rest of the kingdom will turn against us, and all our friends will end up dead."

A high-pitched ringing had started in Katerina's ears. She felt like she was about to pass out.

"Then bargain with her," she replied faintly. "Like Cass said, we can try to make a—"

Dylan shook his head. "It's not going to work—"

"You don't want it to work!"

He flinched as Tanya placed a gentle hand on her arm. Yes, she knew it wasn't at all true. Yes, she knew this was killing him. But the words exploded out of her in the darkest rage.

"You don't *care* if it works, because you don't *care* if we're together, because you were planning on ending it the *second* I took back the crown! What does it matter if you sleep with another woman? It's not like there's anyone holding you back." Another rush of tears poured down her face, and she wiped them away with the back of her hand. "You know what, maybe you should go through with it after all—she'd make a great rebound!"

A look of profound hurt shot across Dylan's face, followed by defensiveness, followed by an anger just as unrestrained as her own.

"Maybe you're right!" he shouted. "Maybe I should!"

"Fine!"

"FINE!"

There was a second where no one moved. A second where the two of them just stared at each other. Pale and shaking. Bursting with all those things they could never say.

Then he turned on his heel and stormed down the hall, vanishing into the darkness the same way as the queen...

What have I done? What did I just do?

Katerina lasted only a second in his absence before falling to her knees. A wave of cold rushed over her, so debilitating and real she wondered if the obsidian itself was leeching every bit of heat from her body. The tears had stopped, but her eyes and lips were wide open. Staring at the place he'd vanished. Praying he would come back. Knowing she would never, *ever* forgive herself.

"Katerina..."

She didn't respond. She didn't even know who'd said her name. Time marched steadily on, but she was scarcely aware it was happening.

She was trapped in that terrible moment. The moment where all hope had vanished, and she'd screamed at him to go.

Eventually, that same voice roused her from the silence.

"Come on."

There was a gentle tug as Cassiel lifted her back to her feet. The darkness behind him was suddenly dotted with torches as the soldiers came back to escort them out of the main hall.

"It's going to be a long night..."

THE CARPATHIAN QUEEN was not nearly as hospitable as she'd pretended to be back in the main hall. Not even to her beloved vampire. The guards took them down a winding set of glass stairs that emptied out into a narrow corridor, as dark and freezing as the first. Without saying a word, they were led to a room at the very end.

Two beds. Two glasses of water. And a window that looked out over nothing.

"Enjoy the view," one of the guards snickered as he backed out into the hall. "I'll come get all of you in the morning, once the queen and your friend have... finished."

The look on Cassiel's face made him retreat in a hurry; the door locked loudly behind him, echoing with a metallic *clank* in the dark. There was the sound of muffled footsteps, a faint pattering on the stairs, then the five friends found themselves alone.

Katerina sank at once onto the nearest mattress. Head in her hands. Silent tears pouring down her face. Imagining she could hear sounds filtering down through the ceiling.

A squeaking bed. A muffled moan. Two sets of shallow breathing.

Tanya took a step towards her, lips opening with words of comfort. Then she thought better of it and went to take one of the glasses of water instead.

"Don't drink that," Aidan advised. "It's been sitting there a long time."

She slowly set it back down. Then gazed out the window instead.

"The *whole* night?" Rose asked quietly, trying to shield the question from Katerina while directing it to Cassiel instead. "She's going to keep him there the *whole* night?"

His eyes tightened with an expression so dark, it didn't seem to fit his lovely face. "One night in exchange for our freedom? I'm sure she sees that as a fair price. And no matter what he's thinking now... Dylan will, too. Eventually."

Tanya stifled a shudder. "Don't say that. Like it's acceptable. Like it's somehow okay—"

"I'm not trying to be callous," he said with strained patience. "I'm trying to see past the horror of the moment. I'm trying to see the bigger picture here—"

"Well, that's just so freakin' wise of you, isn't it, Cass?" Katerina snapped, lifting her head from her hands. "But unlike you, I actually care about Dylan and what's happening to him *now*—"

"You *stupid* girl!" he interrupted viciously. "Of course, I *care* about him! I've cared about him for longer than you've known he was alive—and unlike you, I also care about what he *wants*!"

She flinched, stung by the venom in his voice and the fight in his eyes. There was a reason she took care not to get on Cassiel's bad side. Not the least of which was because he was usually right.

"He doesn't *want* this—" she countered desperately.

"Of course not," he interrupted harshly. There was a beat of silence. "...but he can bear it."

All at once that fire in his eyes disappeared, leaving him tired and bereft in its wake. He sank down onto the mattress beside her, his voice unexpectedly gentle and undeservedly kind.

"Katerina, what he *wants*, more than anything in the entire world, is for you to be safe. If he refused the queen—she would kill you. If he accepts her offer, no matter how deplorable it might be—it gives us a chance. A chance to leave here alive. A chance for you to get back your throne."

Despite the fact that they'd recently been screaming at each other, he took her hand.

"*That's* what he wants," he concluded quietly. "And you can't punish him for it."

She said not a word, just squeezed his fingers. A second later she bowed her head as the tears started up again, crying silently against his arm.

How sweet.

He wants me to have my throne. But he doesn't want his own. He wants to give me a chance to live. But he doesn't care if he kills part of himself in the process. He loves me with all his heart. But he can't see that mine's broken beyond repair.

Note to self... never fall in love with a martyr.

THERE COMES A TIME when, no matter how hard you try to fight against it, exhaustion sets in and the mind simply shuts down.

Katerina was planning on staying awake until sunrise. Counting down the minutes. Living and dying with each one until the endless night was over, and Dylan was set free. If he was upstairs suffering, the least she could do was suffer along with him. She didn't know at what point in the night her body took over. She didn't remember crawling onto the mattress or lying down. The last thing she had any recollection of was Aidan chiding Rose for rattling pointlessly against the door.

Then everything went dark.

Her body aching down to its very bones, Katerina fell into a fitful sleep. Tossing and wincing on the mattress. Plagued by things the others couldn't see. Caught in an endless wave of restless nerves until, all at once, she went frightfully still.

At this point, Tanya discreetly took her pulse and made sure she was still breathing.

The dreams had taken her. And these weren't your run-of-the-mill nightmares. These dreams were fueled by magic. An ancient magic. One that left nothing but scars in its wake.

First, she was back in the courtyard at the Talsing Sanctuary. Standing with a grave-faced Michael as clouds of liquid fire churned in the heavens above. Together, they watched as a young version of Dylan took off his crown, stood up on the ledge and leapt, without thinking, into the sky.

Later, she was walking through a village market. With every step, swarms of different people came out to greet her—all the various creatures she'd met along the road. The succubus barmaid, the frightful old hag that had tried to take her eyes—even the vampires who'd attacked her back at the tavern and again at Pora were there. All cheering. All smiling.

At a glance, it was a happy picture. But as Katerina looked closer, things started to unravel.

The trio of fairies stood on the tips of their toes to see over the crowd, bouncing up and down as they waved, seemingly oblivious to the fact that their wings had caught fire. Katerina tried to warn them, but she was immediately waylaid by a group of laughing children—some with tentacles, some with tails, all of them with chains of daisies strung through their hair.

The princess stared in wonder, then jerked back as the last of the flowery circlets suddenly shook off its petals and transformed into a writhing snake. She let loose a scream, and the little girl wearing it slowly turned around, staring at her with onyx-and-lightning-blue eyes.

The snake bared its teeth, preparing to strike at the child's exposed neck. Katerina sucked in a gasp and was about to grab it, when she was swept into the air by Bernie, her beloved giant. He delightedly waltzed her through the air, trampling different people as he went, ignoring her frantic cries, laughing so loudly it made her ears bleed.

By the time he set her down, there was no village left to trample. Just a sea of broken bodies, their lifeless faces still smiling up towards the sky.

The last dream was the most visceral. And the only one she remembered when she awoke.

She was standing on the banks of a quiet river, the stars twinkling above her, her mother's magic pendant glittering at her throat. For a moment, she simply stood there. Breathing in the cool night air. Soaking in the calm. Then the water at her feet started to ripple, and she looked down to see Alwyn's wrinkled face staring up at her from the waves.

He was smiling, just like the others had been. The same smile she'd seen throughout her entire childhood, so she wasn't sure why, this time, it filled her with dread. He was trying to tell her something, trying to warn her, but his voice was muffled beneath the waves.

Curious, she leaned closer, her mother's pendant slipping out from beneath her dress. It dangled between them over the water, catching every ray of starlight as she tried desperately to hear his frantic words. Then, before her very eyes, the pendant started to glow.

The gem in the middle burned red-hot as the chain that circled her neck started to tighten like a noose. She clawed at it desperately, trying to free herself, but the magic that possessed it was too strong—melting the tips of her fingers, choking off her breath. She tried screaming for help, but it was like Alwyn couldn't hear her. What could he have done anyway, trapped beneath the waves?

The stone itself got heavier and heavier, pulling her down towards the water. Then beneath the water. Then all the way down to the bottom of the river.

She stood on the silty sand, still clawing at the pendant. Still silently screaming. Still staring up in terror as clouds of dark water swirled overhead. Alwyn's face was above her now. He was still smiling, but at the same time he looked profoundly sad. With a heavy hand, he reached down and plucked the necklace off her body, lifting it as though it weighed no more than a charm. The fire cooled as the stone turned black as night, becoming like ash in his wrinkled hand.

There wasn't water churning above her now, there was fire. The entire world had erupted with it—consuming everything in its path. Dylan and Michael at the sanctuary. The group of villagers and the girl with the snake in her hair. The peaceful river and all the twinkling stars.

All of it... was lost to the flames.

Katerina awoke with a gasp. Grabbing fistfuls of the sheets for balance. Head spinning as her body broke out in a cold sweat. So completely disoriented, it took her a second to understand what was going on around her. A second to see that she wasn't the only one in a panic. The others were right there with her as well.

Pounding against the locked door. Sucking in breathless gasps at the window. Screaming for help at the top of their lungs.

That's when Katerina smelled the smoke...

Chapter 13

"What happened? What's going on?" Katerina leapt to her feet, then stumbled back the next second. Pulling her cloak up over her mouth. Choking on the suffocating cloud of smoke that had drifted under the doorway. The others were in similar states of distress. Protecting their faces as much as possible. Squinting against the waves of scorching heat. Pounding against the door and screaming until their hands were bleeding and their voices were hoarse and raw.

"Tanya!" she screamed, catching the girl's arm as she rushed past with the glasses of water, taking a second to splash the cloth tied around everyone's mouths. "What about the window?"

The shape-shifter splashed her, too, then shook her head. Her eyes were wide with fear and red with smoke. "Aidan says it's too far—"

"It's too far down!" the vampire interrupted, sticking his head out as far as it would go and squinting into the shadows. "I can't even see the bottom from here!"

There was a high-pitched help as Rose suddenly shifted, leaving her clothes and weapons in a circle on the floor. Cassiel took an automatic step to the side as the wolf threw her body full-force against the door, rattling it on its hinges. There was a metallic *creak*, but the thing held firm.

"Again," he urged. "As many times as you have to."

She sucked in a ragged breath and nodded once. Throwing herself again and again against the unrelenting metal. Leaving an ever-widening smear of blood in her wake.

"Together," Aidan called, rushing over to help, "on three!"

As the two of them got to work, Cassiel turned in desperation to Katerina. "Got a question for you. Think carefully about the answer. If you were to shift right now, what would happen?"

She froze where she stood, trying to match his breathing. Trying to calm down enough to spare a moment of rational thought. "You would be crushed," she finally said. "All of you."

How she wished it wasn't the answer, but it was true.

There was a reason the friends stood at least fifty feet away from her whenever she attempted to shift. There was a reason she'd recently taken out a small forest of trees. Dragons were enormous, and the transformation was incredibly difficult to control. Even if she did manage to leave her human form behind, there was no way this small chamber would hold her. And she shuddered to think what would happen to her friends—trapped in the same tiny room.

"What if I used my fire?" she asked frantically, clinging with both hands to any semblance of hope. "I could try to get it hot enough to melt the hinges on the door—"

"You want *more* fire in here?" a cheerful voice called out from the window.

The others turned with a gasp to see Dylan dangling effortlessly off the ledge. His clothes were disheveled, but at least he was wearing them. His hands were torn and bloody, but his movements were sure. His face was smudged with soot, but his eyes were bright and dancing.

They swept over each of his friends with a twinkling smile, coming to rest on the princess.

"Let me be the one to say *more* fire seems like a *bad* idea."

Seven hells...

Katerina collapsed back against the wall in relief as the others rushed forward. Cassiel quickly pulled him through the window, while Aidan stuck his head back outside in stunned disbelief.

"How did you do that?" he gasped, staring up at the climb. There were no footholds for the ranger to have used. Nothing but black obsidian glass. "It's impossible."

"Nothing's impossible," Dylan scoffed, looking rather pleased with himself despite their desperate predicament. "A little imagination here, a touch of whimsy there—you'll see the world with brand-new eyes, my friend." Somewhere above them a beam broke, and the gang flinched. "That being said, we have to move. Like... *now.*"

"Any suggestions?" Cassiel clapped him on the back, grinning despite the smoke.

"Out the window, of course."

That smile faded as the fae moved Aidan aside and glanced down for himself.

"Have you lost your—"

"No time to debate, I'm afraid." Dylan started gesturing them forward, looking back out the window himself. "Unless I'm mistaken, a contingent of guards is on their way here right now."

"Well, that's good!" Tanya exclaimed, ignoring the giant wolf still throwing itself against the door behind her. "They'll let us out and—"

"They're coming to watch you burn."

...oh.

With no other options left to them, the gang swiftly gathered around the window. Rose shifted back, scrambling to put on her clothes, but there was no time. Cinders were falling from the ceiling, and the sound of thundering footsteps was getting louder with each passing moment.

"First Cass with Tanya, then Aidan with Rose, then me and Kat," Dylan instructed, calling out the orders like a seasoned general. Whatever strange paralysis had come over him the second they'd stepped into the palace had clearly left. Replaced with that unshakable confidence that had seen them through so much. "Here, take these."

Almost faster than the eye could see, he pressed what looked like a pair of tiny silver blades into Cassiel and Aidan's hands. They were so slender they were hardly noticeable, shaped like the kind of slender prong a woman might use to pull back her hair.

"Shatter the glass, but not too hard," he warned. "They'll let you climb down."

Cassiel clearly had his doubts, but he trusted his friend even more. It wasn't the first time Dylan had told him to jump out a window. It probably wouldn't be the last.

Without a moment's pause, he grabbed Tanya up into his arms and leapt off the ledge. The others could barely hear her high-pitched scream before they vanished into the smoky abyss.

Aidan glanced down after them, looking shaken and pale. "Well, that bodes well..."

Dylan gestured impatiently, and the vampire pulled in a deep breath. A second later he strode across the room and picked up Rose, who was still scrambling to tie on her clothes.

"Ready or not, it's time to leave."

Her eyes narrowed as she wrapped her arms around him, her bare skin pressing up against his chest. "I better not catch you looking, leech."

He chuckled darkly and swung them up onto the ledge. "Trust me, sweetheart," he quipped, gripping the blade in one hand and the shifter in the other, staring down into the clouds of swirling smoke, "you're going to be the last thing on my mind..."

They vanished without a trace. And just like that, only the princess and the ranger remained.

The room was filling with smoke, but for a fleeting moment neither of them moved. There was a crack in that winning façade, and Dylan stared at her cautiously before holding out his hand.

Shall we?"

Same thing he'd said the first time she shifted into a dragon. Same thing he'd said when he asked her to jump off a cliff. Only that time, he'd sealed it with a kiss.

"What happened here?" she whispered hoarsely, her throat stripped raw from the smoke and her eyes tearing with the heat of the fire. "Did you do this?"

For a second, he froze dead still. Then he swept her off her feet with a twinkling smile. "Turns out, I couldn't go through with it after all."

AFTER SCALING DOWN the wall of the palace, with Katerina throwing blazing fireballs at whoever tried to stand in their path, the escape from Carpathia wasn't actually as dramatic as they might have thought. Mostly because, the second they fled there was no one chasing them.

Whatever Dylan had done to escape the queen's chambers clearly had not been contained by the upstairs level of the palace. By the time Katerina and the others made it back to the King's Road, the entire thing was engulfed in flames. A hunk of molten rock blazing against the skyline.

The princess would later learn it had something to do with kerosene. It seemed as though the Carpathian horde hadn't managed to see in the dark after all. The palace was filled with giant vats of the flammable liquid, to supply the torches and fires meant to illuminate the black glass. In an act of what Dylan would only refer to as 'self-preservation,' he'd accidentally knocked a candle into one of these vats and set the thing aflame, unaware at the time that the vats were all connected.

No sooner had he jumped out the window than the entire palace was on fire.

"You don't do things halfway, do you?" Cassiel breathed, turning with the others to gaze back at the building in all its ruined splendor. Heaps of bubbling rock were dripping down the side like a garish popsicle that had been left out too long in the sun.

Dylan stuck his hands in his pockets. "Nope."

The fae shook his head as Katerina shot Dylan a sideways glance. The two hadn't spoken much since their escape through the window, but she found herself unable to contain her smile.

"What happened to not ticking off the Carpathian queen?"

It was impossible to tell whether he blushed, or if it was just the reflection of the flames.

"Who wants allies like that anyway? Besides," he added with a grin, "I know a girl who could torch the whole kingdom with an accidental sneeze. I have to say—I like our odds."

I like our odds, too.

That was the last anyone spoke for a long time. They still had an entire kingdom to flee, and since the massive bonfire was already a dead giveaway to their location the gang had no objection to taking advantage of the smoke cover to expedite their journey.

Just a few minutes after they'd turned their backs on the smoldering palace for the last time, the five friends were soaring away on the back of a dragon. A dragon who snapped menacingly at the circling crows as she soared above the Carpathian wasteland.

Leaving the ashes of the palace behind her. Nothing but the fiery horizon in her eyes.

THE FLYING WAS GETTING easier. The landing was not.

"For FREAK'S SAKE, Katerina!"

She was starting to notice that the fae only referred to her by her full name when he was especially angry. It seemed to be happening more and more.

"I'm sorry!" she cried, crouching naked behind a towering spruce tree. "I really tried that time, I promise!"

He lifted himself off the ground, stiffly, pulling a pair of twigs from his hair. "As opposed to all those other times, when you *don't* try?"

Truth be told, it was kind of fun to mess with him...

"Leave her alone," Dylan chided with a grin, walking towards her hiding place with an outstretched cloak. "You're just lucky she saved us from having to cross that river."

It was true—the crashing river had done nothing to dissipate in the time it took to navigate their way through Carpathia. Soaring at such a high altitude it was easy to see that the raging torrent stretched all the way back to Belaria when, before, it had been just a quiet stream.

There was definitely some darker force at work. But as long as Katerina and the others kept to the skies, there seemed little that force could do to stop them.

"That being said, no more shifting." Dylan held out the cloak without meeting her eyes. "I know it's a convenience, but whether we fly at night or not someone is bound to see, and they're bound to see where you land. It's a fifty-fifty chance as to whether that person is on our side."

Katerina stared at the cloak with a hidden blush. It wasn't the new one he'd gotten from the palace—the one with the embroidered silk and thread. It was his ranger cloak. The one he'd been wearing since they met at the tavern all those months ago. The one that smelled deliciously like the soft leather and pine aroma of his hair. A personal gift—one that meant far more to him to give.

"You can have the other one if you like," he said quietly, reaching for the leather strap across his shoulder. "It's right here in my pack—"

"No," she said quickly, taking it from his outstretched hand. "This is fine. Thank you."

Awkward. No matter how many things they put between them—Carpathian capture, burning down the palace, a midnight flight through the skies—it remained unbearably awkward.

Apparently the others thought so, too. Because, the second Aidan saw the two of them together, he dropped down where he stood and propped a blanket under his head.

"Well, that about does it for me. Even we vampires need to sleep." He motioned for the others to join him before casually calling out to the two who were left. "Kat, Dylan—why don't you guys take the first watch? Rose and I can fill in when you're through."

It was such an obvious ploy, that the princess and the ranger blushed at the same time. Rose, however, seemed to have warmed to the vampire a great deal since their escape out the window.

"Can't get enough, can you?" she teased, running a finger beneath his chin. "Don't beat yourself up about it, Aidan. It happens to most men."

"That's the first time she's called him Aidan," Tanya whispered.

Cassiel nodded, looking mildly impressed. "It's the first time she's called him a man."

Ignoring their friends' silent pleas for help, the four of them shared a conspiratorial grin and settled down for the night, leaving the others out in the cold. In the end, both Katerina and Dylan had no choice but to leave the roaring campfire behind them and set off on their own.

The princess was still fuming about it as they made their way through the trees.

Double-crossing, back-stabbing, bunch of traitorous scum—

"You can go to sleep if you want."

She looked up in surprise to see Dylan staring at her from several yards away. The moonlight had highlighted the smudges of soot streaked across his face, making it look like he'd attempted some kind of poorly-planned nocturnal camouflage.

"It doesn't take the both of us," he continued quietly, staring down at the forest floor with a sheepish flush. "You must be tired."

She appreciated the offer, and a part of her was desperate to take it. But another part was just as capable of standing watch on her own.

"*You* must be tired," she countered, avoiding his gaze as she nervously tucked her hair behind her ears. "I actually got a little sleep last night, while you—" She cut herself off abruptly, horrified by what she'd been about to say. A furious blush burned across her face, and she turned towards the trees to hide it. "I only meant—"

"Nothing happened between me and the queen."

She jerked around with a silent gasp, to see Dylan standing directly behind her. She may be queen of the skies, but he was still king of the forest. No one moved quieter in the trees. Her lips opened, but she had no idea what to say. No idea how to begin to make things right. To apologize.

"The thought of you and she together made me sick," she blurted. *Well... that's one way to start.* The blush spread further but she ignored it, forcing herself to meet his gaze. "I can't...I can't even begin to apologize. Those things I said. Taking *that* moment to come at you with..." Tears slipped down her face, and she quickly wiped them away with the back of her hand. "Dylan, I'm so sorry. I didn't plan it. I didn't mean to say it. It's just... it felt like it was killing me."

The feeling of being torn in half. The feeling of having her heart ripped out by the woman's ice-cold hand... she'd remember it for the rest of her life.

A pair of warm fingers caught her beneath the chin, lifting her head once more. At first, she thought he was going to say something. To either forgive her, hash it out, or simply admit he'd decided to hate her forever. Whatever had happened at the palace— it needed to be addressed.

But he didn't say a word.

He kissed her instead.

"Dylan—" she gasped, but he swept her off her feet. Lifting her gently into his arms, he settled them at the base of a tree.

His hands were urgent, but somehow gentle. Cupping the sides of her face. Stroking back the messy locks of her hair. Winding around the small of her back as the two of them came together.

It was a kiss unlike any the two had shared. A kiss that knew no limits, no boundaries. The stars were out, their friends were asleep, and they had all the time in the world. If it weren't for the fact that Dylan had set them in the middle of a puddle, it could have lasted all night.

"It's really cold..."

Dylan pulled back in surprise as Katerina bit her lip, shivering. "What?"

It was then his eyes found the freezing pool of water he'd settled her in. It was then he registered the icy sludge himself, seeping up through the fabric on his legs.

"Crap—sorry!" He lifted her at once, glancing about quickly for a drier bed of leaves. Then he bowed his head, quiet chuckling, spilling his dark hair into his eyes. "We can never get a break, can we?"

She stared at him for a long moment, then they started laughing at the same time.

Once it started, they couldn't get it to stop. Their bodies quaked and trembled as they finally just embraced it. Leaning into each other for support. Trying helplessly to mask the sound with their hands. Letting it sweep over them in endless waves, until at long last they both fell silent.

When it was finished, they stood there for a long time. She was still in his arms—he'd never even considered putting her down—yet the two of them were in their own little worlds. Thinking about what had happened in the last twenty-four hours. Trying to piece it all together. Thoughtfully considering their own parts and wondering what was going to happen next.

"It made me sick, too," he finally said.

Katerina's head jerked up and she found him staring at her with soft, gentle eyes. "It did?"

He nodded silently, arms squeezing subconsciously tighter around her body. "At first, I thought I could handle it. Just grit my teeth and... it was only for a few hours." A tremble ran through his body as he slowly lifted his gaze. "I thought I could pretend she was you."

Silent tears streaked down Katerina's face, absorbed in his cloak.

"I should have known that would never work," he continued softly. "The two of you couldn't be less alike. And when she started..." He trailed off with eyes so lost and bleak, Katerina knew she'd remember them forever. "I was about to leave. About to tell her to throw me in the cell with the rest of you. But then the strangest thing happened... I started smiling."

As desolate as his face had become, it was just as radiant now. Shining with an inner brilliance that seemed to light up the darkness around him.

Katerina blinked. "You started *smiling*?"

"I know," he laughed softly, "I was pretty surprised myself. Anyway, she asked me why I was smiling, and it was because, in that moment, I had suddenly realized the truth. In that moment, I suddenly realized I would do anything in the world to get back to you."

Katerina's breath froze in her chest as her eyes locked onto his face.

"Whether that meant ticking off the queen, or burning down the whole of Carpathia." There was a hitch in his breathing, and he looked up at her with enormous, breathtaking eyes. "Whether it meant taking up my father's crown... I would do it all. To be with you."

Their eyes met, and the rest of the world seemed to fade away.

"I'm in *love* with you, Katerina. Now and forever. There is no stopping point for me. There is no amount of time that will suddenly be enough." One hand clasped hers, holding it close to his chest. "There is no enough. I am yours, and you are mine. Nothing will ever change that."

A day that had started in a nightmare ended in a dream.

Katerina kissed him once on the lips. Sweetly, chastely. Then dropped her head back and closed her eyes. Memorizing his exact words. Memorizing the exact look on his face when he said them. Several seconds went by before a set of fingers stroked the side of her cheek. She didn't need to be looking to see the dimpled grin.

"What are you thinking?"

She opened her eyes with a smile, staring up at the stars. "That the two of us are really bad at breaking up..."

Chapter 14

Katerina rolled over in her sleep and felt a warm hand slip inside her pocket, fingers sliding over the weathered fabric stretched across her hip. A sleepy grin curved her lips as she cuddled closer into Dylan, reaching back and pulling his arm around her like a blanket.

Only...his arm wasn't there.

Her eyes shot open, and she found herself face to face with a man who looked nothing like her handsome boyfriend. This man was in his fifties. He had wide-set green eyes, an enormous hooked nose, and a crooked tooth that peeked out from between his lips.

He was currently rifling around in her pocket.

"What the—"

She bolted up with a gasp at the same time that Dylan open his eyes on the ground beside her. He'd been lying on his back, one hand reaching towards hers, a look of peaceful contentment on his face. All that changed when he saw the stranger rifling around in his jacket.

"HEY!"

In a flash, he was on his feet. Kicking out at the man while pulling Katerina safely behind him. His boot made contact, and the man who'd been assaulting her landed with an almost comedic *thud* right on his behind. His friends scattered, but he stayed where he was. Blinking in astonishment at the two teenagers. Looking almost as surprised as they were themselves.

"How did you move that fast?" the thief asked.

The question threw Dylan, and he came to a sudden pause. He had questions of his own, of course. Mainly—who the heck were these people, and what did they think they were doing? But there was something so disarmingly defenseless about the man, it caught him off guard.

"I just..." He shook his head with frustration and started again. "I don't need to answer to you, old man! Why the heck were you digging through our clothes?!"

Clothes—some of those would be nice...

Katerina clutched Dylan's cloak tighter around her body. She'd yet to get dressed after shifting back into her human form, and it was the only thing protecting her from the outside world.

For a second, the awkward trio simply stood there. Staring each other down. Trying to process what had happened. Then a flash of sudden understanding lit the man's bulging eyes.

"Oh... you're a shifter." He pushed casually to his feet, dusting himself off in the process. "I wouldn't have tried if I'd known you were a shifter. Sorry for the mistake."

With that, he flashed them a cheerful smile. As if he couldn't possibly fathom why they were still staring at him with looks of shock. It wasn't until they heard distant shouting coming from deeper in the woods that he had the decency to blush.

"Oh, dear..."

Dylan and Katerina paled with an incredulous sort of rage, but before they were able to say a word the shouting started again. Some voices they recognized. Some they didn't.

"Dylan! Dylan, get your arse over here!"

That was Cassiel.

Without a look behind him, Dylan was off like a shot. Pausing only long enough to throw a quick, "Kat, you got him?" over his shoulder.

The princess saluted, then whipped out her knife and cocked her head towards the trees with a sweet smile. "After you."

The man nodded his head sadly, clutching his hat in his hands. "Yes... I'm afraid so."

BY THE TIME KATERINA and the stranger made their way through the trees, the situation had changed dramatically. The others had already set aside their differences with the thirty or so people who had invaded their camp. More than that, they were in the process of sharing a hearty breakfast.

"Kat!" Tanya called cheerfully by the fire, waving a stick with a skewered sausage. "Come get something to eat!"

The princess slowly lowered her knife as she and the man gazed around the encampment with varying degrees of amusement and disbelief. After a moment, he clapped her sympathetically on the shoulder and cocked his head towards the fire with a twinkling smile.

"Coffee or tea?"

She blinked, stared around for a second more, then sheathed the blade with a helpless shrug. "Tea, please." Despite the fact that the man had been in the process of robbing them not five minutes before, almost two decades of manners clicked in and she added a hasty, "Uh, thank you, Mister...?"

"Callahan," he said brightly, tipping his hat with a little bow. "Reginald Callahan."

"Right," Katerina said faintly as he made his way over to the others. "Callahan." She watched as he disappeared into the crowd, then slowly rotated to take in the rest.

If she didn't know better, she would have sworn the lot of them were fast friends.

Cassiel was the one who had shouted, and although his cloak was crumpled on the ground with a bloody arrow beside it, he was talking animatedly to a man about half his size. A man who was sporting a similarly bloody arm but didn't seem all that bothered by it. Tanya had a stray-like tendency to be forever loyal to those who provided her with food. Rose was sporting some brand-new leather clothes and was proudly showing them off to a group of admirers. Even Aidan, the most standoffish of the group, was speaking to an old man with obvious interest, pausing every now and then to sip from a flagon of what looked like blood.

"Gypsies."

She startled in surprise, then cast a sideways glance over her shoulder as Dylan came up to stand beside her. He wasn't exactly as enthusiastic as the others, but at least there was nothing overtly aggressive in the way he folded his arms and gazed out over the proceedings.

"I don't care who they are," the princess began quietly. "They were *stealing* from us."

Dylan shrugged, as if these things were hardly avoidable. "They tried."

She rolled her eyes, unwilling to surrender the point. "Yeah, Dylan, they *tried*."

He glanced at her quickly, then suppressed a grin. A second later he was leading her by the shoulders towards a nearby bluff, one that gazed out over the valley below.

"The thing about gypsies," he explained as they walked, "is that they're immensely loyal, but they also carry a grudge. You're either family or an enemy. There's nothing in between."

Katerina glanced behind her as they hiked up through the trees. "So? I can carry a grudge, too. And when I woke up, that guy had his hands in my cloak."

He pursed his lips as they neared the top. "The other thing about gypsies is that they tend to travel in large groups." They came to a stop and he angled her to the valley. To the hundreds of people camped below. "*Very* large groups."

Holy moly!

Katerina's mouth fell open in astonishment as she stared over the side of the bluff. Caravan was too small a word for it. What she was seeing looked as if an entire village had uprooted and taken to the road. A sea of colorful tents and wagons stretched across the valley floor. Tents teeming with so many sights and sounds and smells, she was having trouble deciding where to look first.

Children roved in little packs of laughter, sprinting delightedly on muddy trails while studiously avoiding their parents' call. Women greeted each other warmly as they emerged from their tents with buckets of laundry or baskets of food, preparing to go about their morning tasks. Men sat about in self-important circles, trying to out-do each other telling stories, smoking cigars, or dredging up old memories.

It was the kind of sight that would have been strictly banned from her at the castle. The kind of sight that had earned a permanent place in her heart.

But here... there were *so many* of them.

"You're either family or you're an enemy, huh?" she breathed, watching as more and more people flooded up the path towards their camp. "So, what does that mean for us?"

Dylan's lips quirked up as he playfully elbowed her in the ribs. "It means we smile..."

BACK IN THE CAMPSITE breakfast was underway, and Reginald Callahan was waiting patiently with the princess' tea. He hurried over the second he spotted her, clumsily splashing it in his hands.

"There you are." He passed it to her with a warm smile. "I couldn't see where you'd gone."

She accepted it with a deliberate smile of her own, determined to make up for their rather rocky start. The tea was rich and spicy, brewed with herbs she'd never seen before. "I was just looking over your camp. It's huge." She tilted her head to the side, casually pressing for more information. "There have to be over a hundred people down there."

Reginald nodded, taking a scalding sip for himself. "Closer to two hundred, actually. We met up with another camp near Bainsfort, and I doubt it will be the last. Everyone's headed down to—"

"Reggie!" The man looked up suddenly then took a step back, making way for the tall man who'd just strode into their midst. "Why don't you introduce me to your new friends?"

It only took a glance to see this was the man in charge.

Not only was he a bit taller than the others, but he was a bit sharper. Moving through the crowd with a confident ease, while avoiding the pockets of pleasant conversation that had popped up throughout the camp. His gaze carefully took in Dylan and Katerina, the same way he'd done with the others, before the caution vanished and he extended his hand with a warm smile.

"Greetings, friends!" he said cheerfully. "What a pleasure it is running into you this fine morning! And so far into the woods! We hadn't expected to see anyone for hours."

Dylan stepped forward to greet him, accepting his hand. "The pleasure is ours."

Katerina quickly followed . She had never seen Dylan so friendly. Truth be told, she had never seen him friendly at all. But there was a caution beneath the words. A guarded readiness behind the smile. It was a game these two were playing. A game neither one was willing to lose.

The handshake was brief, but firm. More of a sizing up than a greeting. Still, the smiles remained the same. In a world prone to violence and death, they were the best defense.

"Just passing through?"

The man offered no name, and Dylan certainly didn't volunteer one. Not that it seemed to matter. Both men seemed determined to be pleasant no matter the cost.

"On our way to Rocburrough." Dylan gestured with a vague tilt of his head. "Then we'll keep heading south to the Dells. My brother has a farm there. We're hoping to find work."

Katerina resisted the urge to punch him in the ribcage.

Family farm, huh? Wonder where you got that excuse.

"The Dells," the man repeated, his dark eyebrows shooting up into his hair. "That's a long way. Over a month's journey from here."

A month in the wrong direction. The six of them had been heading due west.

"Are you sure you have everything you need?" he pressed. "Running low on supplies?"

This time, the smile Dylan flashed seemed genuine. He rested his hands casually on his hips, incidentally opening his jacket enough to reveal both the knife and the bag of coins beneath.

"Actually, there *are* some things that we need…"

Just like that, the game was over and both men conceded in peace. No, the gypsy horde would not take what they wanted by force. Even if their numbers would have made it easy. And no, Dylan and the others would not leave them empty-handed. The gypsies had shared their food, shared their drink, and were rather cheerfully sparing their lives. Whether the gang needed supplies or not, they would certainly be leaving behind some money in their wake.

The man clapped his arm around Dylan's shoulders, and the two of them headed off towards the wagons. No one but the princess noticed the way Cassiel's hand casually released his dagger as they walked past. A burly man standing beside the fire discreetly sheathed his knife.

TWO HOURS LATER, THE gang had significantly dented the funds they'd brought with them from Belaria and found themselves overwhelmed with an array of things they didn't really need. At least, the men didn't seem to think they needed them. The women were of a slightly different opinion.

"Take a look at this!" Tanya whipped an iridescent dagger out of her belt and held it up proudly. "Double-sided Matlaen steel. Collapsible, so I can store it in my boot, and capable of flying at speeds up to a hundred and fifty miles per hour from a seasoned hand." She flipped it expertly in the air before catching it by the blade. "*And* it's supposed to change color based on my mood."

The men, who had been listening with interest thus far, rolled their eyes in disgust.

"Oh, yeah?" Rose looked her over with a fond smile. "What does orange mean?"

The tiny shifter's face fell as she gazed after the departing caravan. "I don't know. The man who sold it to me didn't say..." She was quiet for a moment before her eyes lit up with their usual charisma. "I think it means I'm excited."

Rose laughed before turning to Katerina. "I bet you didn't get anything, right, princess?" she quipped. "Why would you? You'll have everything you'll ever need back at that castle of yours."

There was an odd strain beneath the words, but the princess didn't notice. She was too busy holding court with new weapons of her own.

"Are you kidding?" A grin stretched from ear to ear as she twirled around a pair of sai. "It's going to be a whole new chapter. A little more... hands-on, you could say."

Rose melted into the background, watching her carefully as Tanya gave her new dagger another magnificent spin, barely missing Dylan in the process.

"What about you, your canine lordship? What are you planning to do when all this is over?"

She scarcely remembered the heated undertones of the question, especially in light of the recent fight, but just as the others nervously glanced over Katerina answered with a beaming smile. "Dylan's going back to Belaria."

The effect this had on the group was overwhelming. Rose and Tanya let loose their instant approval. Aidan offered the king a rare smile. And Cassiel looked like at least a decade lost to frustration had been added back onto his life.

"You are?" he asked, watching his friend carefully for any signs of doubt. "Really?"

Dylan nodded slowly but kept his eyes on Katerina. "Belaria... that's a long way from the High Kingdom."

"Are you kidding?" She tossed him a wink. "I can make that flight in under an hour."

A strange look came over Dylan's face, a vague surprise, as if he hadn't yet put two and two together. The others laughed when they saw it as Cassiel clapped him supportively on the back.

"That's right. You're officially dating a dragon." His eyes teemed with mischief. "You'll have to hang up that sword for good."

Katerina shot him a sour look, not entirely convinced the sword wasn't metaphorical. Tanya seemed to suspect to so, because she looked her boyfriend up and down with a shrewd eye.

"Just like you, babe?" she asked in a dangerously sweet voice.

There was a guilty pause.

"Of course, darling."

Rose took the moment to wisely intercede. "What about you, Tanya? What are you going to do when all this is finished?"

The shifter shrugged, planning it out on the fly—the way she did with most major life decisions. "Not sure. I suppose Cass and I will probably hang around the High Kingdom for a while. Collecting medals, breeding horses, throwing banquets in our name... then I suppose we can go to Belaria and do the same thing."

Katerina turned with a grin to Cassiel, unaware that he had frozen perfectly still. "And you, Cass? You have big plans for medal-collecting and horse-breeding?"

The fae paled slightly before giving a dismissive shrug. Avoiding his girlfriend's eyes. "I...I hadn't really given it much thought."

The handle on Tanya's dagger changed color.

"And you?" Katerina shifted the conversation quickly, turning to Rose instead. "Are you going to be settling down in the High Kingdom?"

Secretly, she hoped all of them would. Secretly, she was already thinking of them as her High Council. But it looked as though that plan wasn't going to be as easy as she'd thought...

"I'm not sure..." A look of profound hesitation clouded Rose's beautiful face, along with a flash of vulnerability the others rarely saw. "I was planning on it. But now... I don't know. It might be nice to go back to a place like Pora for a while. Help the rebels there relocate. Start rebuilding their lives..."

The answer surprised Katerina, then it didn't. Despite the flashy show she put on for the others, there was something inherently thoughtful about Rose. A deep current of empathy lay buried beneath all the rest. Guiding her actions. Making her unintentionally sweet, even when she tried to present herself as careless and strong.

"They'd be lucky to have you," the princess said with a smile. "So would I," she added quickly, "if you decided to come back and stay."

Rose's eyes flashed, full of that same profound hesitation. But before she could say a word the trees opened up behind her as the last of the gypsies headed out on the road.

"Well, I'm afraid this is goodbye." Reginald Callahan, the worst thief there ever was, gave each of the friends a parting wave before leaning down and spontaneously kissing Katerina on the cheek. "Sorry about the other thing. You know... before."

"You mean when you were feeling us up in our sleep?" Dylan asked innocently, pulling his girlfriend back to his side. He and the man locked eyes for a chilling moment, then he laughed softly. "Don't worry about it."

Reggie exhaled loudly in relief before chuckling along with him. He waved a cheerful goodbye, but before he left he turned back to Katerina one last time.

"You know, it's the funniest thing. We heard reports that someone saw a dragon touch down here last night. Can you believe it? A real-life dragon."

Their eyes met, and for a split second Katerina saw that Reggie wasn't nearly as bumbling and clueless as he might seem. Strangely enough, it made her like him even more.

"We actually heard that, too. Better be careful." She leaned in with an angelic smile. "A real-life dragon? There's no telling *what* the thing might do..."

He laughed a deep rumbling laugh before throwing a satchel over his shoulder. "I'm sure it wouldn't have any concern for little old me. At any rate, the caravan's going to be as far away from these parts as possible. We're heading over to the High Kingdom."

"The High Kingdom?" Katerina's playful façade fell away as she stared at the man with open concern. "Why on earth are you people heading there?"

Reggie looked vaguely surprised that she would have to ask.

"It's the prince's coronation, of course. Why do you think we've packed those wagons to the gills? It's going to be a five-kingdom-wide party. Lots to see. Lots to sell."

Without another word, he gave them one last wave and disappeared over the bluff with the last of his friends.

The princess stayed rooted to the spot where he'd left her. Hands clenching into fists. Eyes flashing with unspeakable rage.

"Kat..." Dylan approached her cautiously, laying a gentle hand on her arm. "I know what you must be thinking; I know that look. But it's *crucial* that we don't panic here or do anything stupid that we might regret—"

"Regret? Of course not." She shook him off with a humorless smile, her grey eyes fixing like storm clouds on the distant horizon. "You heard the man—it's a *party*, Dylan. A coronation party."

Those fists of hers turned into flames.

"I think we might just have to stop by."

IT HAD TAKEN AN HOUR to reason with her friends. Another hour after that to get the fae on board. These people weren't used to making rash decisions, especially at this stage of the game, and despite the reasoning behind Katerina's actions they were extremely hesitant to endorse the plan.

But in the end, the princess' logic was inescapable.

Kailas was about to be crowned king. After that happened it wouldn't just be an act of rebellion to stand against him, it would be an act of treason. An act punishable by death.

It was precisely the reason he'd moved up the ceremony. It was precisely the reason Katerina had to stop it now. She'd wanted to do it properly. March on the castle with an army willing to fight for her cause. But she was unwilling to raise those stakes so high. Not when she knew so many of the faces fighting for her. Not when there was a dark wizard on the other side.

The second the debate was over, things happened very quickly.

Dylan ran down to the valley and caught up with the gypsy caravan. Once there, he purchased four messenger ravens and hurried back. Tiny scrolls were written out in a careful hand, saying what they intended to do and putting their allies, spread out across the map, on standby.

The first was sent to Michael.

Katerina didn't know exactly why she thought this one was necessary. The man was politically neutral and was one of the only people they'd met who hadn't pledged people and support to their cause. But it made her feel better, knowing that he was in the loop. There was something unshakably steady about the man. He radiated an almost omniscient kind of wisdom. Between that and the fact that Dylan was the one to have suggested it, his was the first letter she wrote.

The raven took to the sky. Followed quickly by another.

This one went out to Petra, the unofficial leader of the rebel camps. In a way, they were all very glad to be sending a raven with their news and not delivering it in person. No one more so than Aidan. Not only had they taken a massive detour—crowning Dylan in Belaria after soaring on the wings of a dragon across the night sky—but they'd never managed to get to Rorque, their main objective. Most might argue that they'd exceeded the mission's every goal, but Katerina had a feeling that Petra wasn't really one for spontaneity. But they would deal with the fallout later. In the meantime, she would rally the remaining camps and forces in case they were to fail.

The third raven was sent to Atticus Gail—informing him of the plan and requesting that he have the army at the ready. On the bottom of this note Dylan scribbled a hasty message not to worry, that the plan wasn't really as dangerous as it seemed. And the fourth was sent to Alwyn.

To Katerina's extreme surprise, Rose had been staunchly against the last message. According to her, sending a bird carrying their plan straight into the High Kingdom was akin to suicide. She might have been right. But Alwyn was the only ally she had within the castle. Their one and only inside man. An inside man who happened to be one of the world's most powerful wizards. Katerina would be a fool if she didn't press every advantage she could possibly get. Especially one as invaluable as that.

So, the four birds shot into the air, each flying in a separate direction. East to the Talsing Sanctuary, south to Pora, north to Belaria, and west to the High Kingdom. The friends stared after them for a moment before Katerina started packing up her things.

"Come on," she said quietly. "We don't have much time."

Without a word, the camp was broken down. The fire was put out. The weapons were streamlined. And the things they wouldn't be carrying were hidden safely in the trees. Rose was just passing Cassiel his bow and arrow, when Katerina finished the last of it herself.

"All right, this is it. The point of no return."

She looked at each of them in turn, weighing each word with the utmost care. "I want to thank you. Every single one of you, for everything you've done. It's the kind of thing I can't really put into words..."

She trailed off, forbidding the tears to fall.

"You've all saved my life—more than once. You've risked everything to be here, and now I'm asking you to risk it all again. Just once more. One more time... and then we can give this world the future it deserves. Not suffering at the hand of a despot. But thriving. Coexisting. Giving each man, woman, and child the chance to live as they should. To live in the open. Safe and free."

Five pairs of eyes stared back at her. Bright with determination. Hard as nails. She met each one of them before turning to the last pair. A staggering sky-blue. Staring back with a twinkle.

"So that's it, I guess. Are we ready?"

The friends nodded silently, then made their way to the edge of the clearing.

Katerina turned around, dropped her cloak, and closed her eyes. Touched her neck where the pendant used to hang. Said a little prayer. Then she lifted her arms and vanished into thin air.

A fiery dragon rose up in her place.

IT WAS A GOOD THING the friends had spent so long lingering in the woods. By the time they crossed the border of the High Kingdom, darkness had already begun to fall. Katerina stayed as close to the ground as she could, the tips of her wings skimming across the soft grass and gentle waters that blanketed the land. The outer rim was mostly uninhabited, and on the rare occasion that someone did look up the princess was already gone. They attributed it to a bird, or a shadow. Or simply a trick of the imagination as they went about their nightly chores.

When she got to the forest that bordered the castle, the one where she'd made her wild escape just months ago, she descended into the dark trees, touching down soundlessly as close to the main road as she could. The five friends scrambled off her back, and just moments later she was standing among them. Wearing the clothes that Tanya had carried for her. A whole host of weapons strapped to her side.

"We stick together." Dylan spoke so quietly that the rest of them had to lean closer, reading his lips. "No matter what—no one goes off on their own. Agreed?"

They others nodded, and Katerina shivered as she adjusted the strap of her pack.

The last time she'd been in these trees she'd been barefoot. Dressed in nothing but a nightgown. No one to help her. A pair of raging hellhounds nipping at her heels.

How different things were now. And yet, they felt eerily the same.

Six people to infiltrate an entire castle? What was I thinking?

"Kat."

She glanced up to see Dylan staring at her. The others were already waiting at the bottom of the trail. His eyes swept her over with practiced efficiency before he reached down to take her hand.

"You ready?"

She stared at him for a fleeting moment, then laced her fingers through his. "Yeah. I am."

For the first time in all the various places they'd traveled, Katerina led the way. This forest was as familiar to her as the back of her own hand. The place where she and Kailas had played together as children. She knew its tricks. She knew its tracks.

They made good time to the tree line, then came to a sudden stop. Crouching behind the shrubbery in the darkness, they watched the parade of guards circle the base of the castle.

"I count about thirty," Aidan whispered. "We can probably take them, but not before one of them raises the alarm. If you'd like, I can try to—"

"We're not going in that way," Katerina interrupted. The others turned to her curiously as she dug around in a pile of overgrown holly, then pried open a rusted door. "We're going in *this* way."

It was the same tunnel she'd used to escape. The one that opened up behind a picture of the prince and princess at the end of an upstairs hall.

"Yeah..." Tanya said approvingly, "that'll work."

The others vanished into the darkness without a second's pause, while Dylan gave Katerina a swift look. Perhaps he was the only one to notice the strips of shredded holly still strewn about the forest floor from her desperate flight. Perhaps he was just the best at reading her face.

"Speaking from personal experience?"

She grabbed his hand again, holding it tightly as she scrambled into the eerie tunnel along with the rest of them. "This whole thing is speaking from personal experience..."

THE FIRST TIME KATERINA had come down the tunnel—sprinting as fast as she could the other direction—it had felt endless. The cold had leeched into her body, strings of underground dampness clung to her hair, and she'd been so frightened it felt as though she couldn't breathe.

It was a slightly different experience today.

"Whoa, Kat! You're getting good at that!"

Tanya skipped gleefully forward to stand by the princess' side, gazing fearlessly into the retreating darkness as it vanished before Katerina's flaming hands.

At first, Katerina wasn't sure the fire would even work. She'd tried summoning it in desperate situations many times before, but it usually failed. But there was something different about the way she felt tonight. Despite the danger all around her, despite the dreadful bleakness of her homecoming, she was strangely calm. As if she'd taken some kind of sedative just moments before.

The flames whipped and danced around them in the dark, vanishing suddenly as they came to the closed door on the other side. It was here that they paused, huddling together.

"So, remember, this is a surgical strike. We're going to get Kailas and get out. Kill no more guards than we have to. Stay no longer than is absolutely required."

It was the princess who gave the instructions this time, Dylan standing tall by her side.

Of course, there was a lot she wasn't saying. For example, she'd refused to let herself think about what exactly it meant to 'get' Kailas. No matter what he'd done, what he planned to do, she didn't relish the thought of killing her only brother. Simply extracting him would do for now.

Even if killing him is eventually required...

She pushed the dark thought from her mind and gestured to the door. "They have far fewer guards inside than out, but there's still no way of knowing what's waiting for us on the other side."

At this point, Dylan took over.

"Aidan and I will go first. Cass can cover with arrows just behind. Rose and Tanya, you two cover the princess. And for bloody sake, Katerina, please try to keep out of sight."

"Sure. Out of sight," she agreed quickly.

Yeah, that's not going to happen.

There was a silent countdown, and on three the door swung open and the six friends leapt out of the darkness and into the light...

...only to find a small company of soldiers waiting on the other side.

Apparently, the prince wasn't taking any chances with security before his big day.

For a second, everyone froze. Then a controlled sort of chaos broke out.

Aidan leapt upon the first two guards with no weapons whatsoever, burying his fangs in their necks in a flash of shadowy speed. Dylan took down three more in a blinding array of flashing metal—trying out his new gypsy weapons for the first time—while Cassiel perched upon the open ledge and felled at least six more with arrows.

It was an impressive show of strength, but not nearly as impressive as what happened next.

There was a lone guard coming up from a side hall. A guard no one had seen, but who had certainly seen Katerina. He lifted his hands with a shout and let loose a handful of daggers, aiming each one for the princess' throat. The men froze, too far away to help, and Katerina watched in what felt like slow motion as the deadly blades flew her away.

Except... they never got there.

Katerina didn't actually see Rose move. She simply felt a rush of air as the shifter sprinted past her. One second, she was running along the floor. The next, it looked like she was flying.

A cloud of dark hair whipped around her as she flipped and spun and twirled in a straight path towards the guard. Kicking the blades aside as she went. Snatching others right out of the air. Moving with such impossible, effortless precision, that the man was still standing there, slack-jawed, when she landed right in front of him.

In signature Rose fashion, she flashed him a dazzling smile before plunging those daggers she'd been collecting straight into his chest. He fell without a word. Still trying to reconcile what had happened. Leaving the others just as stunned.

Seven hells...

Katerina blinked in amazement as she realized a sudden truth. Randall and his band of thugs hadn't backed away from her that day at the monastery because Rose was a friend. They'd backed away because they knew the shifter could tear them from limb to limb.

"Thank you," she murmured as the girl tossed back her hair and returned to the others. "I can't believe you just... thank you."

"Don't mention it." Rose flashed her a tight smile as she pocketed the remaining daggers to keep for herself. "Can't let anything happen to you—you're kind of the glue around here." She gave Katerina the remaining dagger before adding suddenly, "I've never been the glue to anyone."

The sudden admission seemed to surprise them both, and Katerina softened with instinctual sympathy as she stared at her. This coming from the girl who'd tried to teach herself how to apologize on the sanctuary roof. This coming from the girl who'd done nothing but protect and serve since the moment she sat down to help Katerina build that bridge.

"You are to us," she said quietly as the others began to move with swift synchronicity down the abandoned hallway. "I'm serious, Rose, thank you—"

The shifter shot her a strained look, then fell in line with the others. "Katerina, *really*... don't mention it."

Not another word was spoken until they reached the upper levels, and not another guard was seen. By the time they made it to Kailas' chambers on the top floor a sinking feeling had settled in Katerina's gut.

This was too easy. We should have had a harder time.

The others were moving with similar caution. None more so than Dylan as he reached carefully for the door. He pulled it open in one swift movement, and the others leapt inside.

Weapons raised. Braced for whatever was to come.

But the prince wasn't there. The room was abandoned. The closet was empty, the bed was made. In fact, it looked as though it had been abandoned for quite a long time.

Katerina stared around in shock, gazing at the tidy room. The Kailas she remembered was never tidy. Since he was just a kid, the guy liked to make a mess. There wasn't a single childhood memory she had when this place wasn't covered in clothes, or books, or weapons. It had become the castle joke; the maids used to hate coming here. But now?

A sudden clatter against the far wall made her jump.

Maybe not so abandoned after all.

Dylan flew towards the curtains, and the next second he reemerged—holding a terrified-looking servant by the arm. The young man's eyes flew around the room before landing on the princess with genuine fear. He struggled and gasped, but Dylan held him firm.

"Where's the prince?" he asked between gritted teeth. "Where's Kailas?"

"H-he's not here," the man stammered frightfully, keeping his eyes locked on Katerina. "I haven't seen him in a long time. They just sent me up to light some candles—"

"I don't care about the candles, I care about the prince," Dylan growled. "If he isn't here, then where is he? With all the guards stationed outside, I know he's in the castle."

The man kept silent only until Dylan gave him a threatening shake.

"He's in the dungeons," he cried. "But that's all I know. I swear!"

Dylan stared down at him in disgust before knocking him out with a single punch. The servant crumpled to the floor as he turned back to Katerina. "Why would he be there?"

"I don't know," she replied, still looking at the servant. "Probably torturing prisoners for information. Let's go."

They left without another word, keeping to the shadows as they crept down a lower staircase to the torchlit levels that travelled beneath the ground. Katerina hadn't been able to shake the sinking feeling in her stomach; it was getting worse with ever step. By the time they made it down to the dungeon itself she was trying very hard not to tremble.

"No guard," Dylan breathed as they approached the door. "Why would there be no guard?"

The others shared an uneasy look but had no answer as they hovered in the darkened corridor, just a stone's throw away from their prize.

"Maybe we should..." Rose started to speak, but her throat closed up and she glanced helplessly back the way they'd come. "Maybe we should come back with more people. Just wait—"

"We can't turn back now," Tanya whispered. "Same plan as before. We're in, we're out. We stay here no longer than necessary. Right?"

Aidan nodded silently as Katerina pulled in a deep breath. "Right."

Another silent countdown, and the door flew open.

This time, it took a second for Katerina's eyes to adjust to the lack of light. It was dark enough in the adjoining corridor, but the entire dungeon was lit only by a few thin candles. The air was thick, smelling of stale water and blood, and unless Katerina's eyes were deceiving her the doors to every cell were hanging wide open. Every cell, except the one at the very end.

For a second, the world stood still. Then Cassiel staggered backwards with a gasp.

"Sera!"

The princess looked on in shock as he went tearing forward, leaving the others without a second thought. They froze for a moment before sprinting after him—calling out words of surprise and warning, skidding to a stop just as suddenly as he had at the end of the corridor.

It was impossible to describe the expression on his face. Katerina had never seen anyone so destroyed, and beautiful, and gutted, and breathlessly relieved all at the same time.

Except perhaps the girl staring back at him.

"Cassiel?" She slowly lifted herself from the wet floor of the cell, approaching the bars cautiously with wide, luminous eyes. "Is this real? Am I dreaming?"

Tears streaked down his face as he reached through the bars, grabbing her small, trembling hands and enclosing them in his own. "I can't believe it," he gasped, unable to catch his breath. "I thought you were dead. This whole time, I thought..."

A wave of emotion overwhelmed him, and he pressed her bruised knuckles against his forehead, openly crying at the touch. There was a movement beside Katerina as Dylan drifted past her. Eyes wide and staring. Completely undone.

"Serafina?" He looked as though he couldn't believe it. Even with her standing just inches away. Even as his fingers reached out of their own accord to touch the back of her hand. "I don't understand. How is this..."

A faint sound echoed through the dark, making them all jump. Dylan turned around at the same time that Cassiel lifted his head, staring wide-eyed into the shadows.

It was then that Katerina saw him. Standing with his back against the wall. Looking exactly as she remembered. Just as tall, just as handsome. Eyes piercing the dark.

Her twin brother.

Kailas.

THE END

Boundless
The Final Chapter...

Boundless Blurb:

MAGIC RUNS THICKER than blood...

As the final battle approaches, the exiled princess finally returns home...only to find that things are not as they seem.

After a shocking discovery leaves them scrambling, Katerina and the gang find themselves faced with the toughest problem yet—finding an enemy they can kill. Alliances are tested, traitors are revealed, and bonds are stretched to the brink as the two armies march towards each other.

Can Katerina find a way to save the one person she thought was already lost? Can she unlock the secrets of her family's ancient power in time? Or will she find herself losing more than just a crown and a kingdom?

Only time will tell.

The Queen's Alpha Series

Eternal
Everlasting
Unceasing
Evermore
Forever
Boundless

Find W.J. May

Website:
http://www.wanitamay.yolasite.com
Facebook:
https://www.facebook.com/pages/Author-WJ-May-FAN-PAGE/141170442608149
Newsletter:
SIGN UP FOR W.J. May's Newsletter to find out about new releases, updates, cover reveals and even freebies!
http://eepurl.com/97aYf

More books by W.J. May

The Chronicles of Kerrigan

BOOK I - *Rae of Hope* **is FREE!**

Book Trailer:

http://www.youtube.com/watch?v=gILAwXxx8MU

Book II - *Dark Nebula*

Book Trailer:

http://www.youtube.com/watch?v=Ca24STi_bFM

Book III - *House of Cards*

Book IV - *Royal Tea*

Book V - *Under Fire*

Book VI - *End in Sight*

Book VII – *Hidden Darkness*

Book VIII – *Twisted Together*

Book IX – *Mark of Fate*

Book X – *Strength & Power*

Book XI – *Last One Standing*

BOOK XII – *Rae of Light*

PREQUEL –
  Christmas Before the Magic
  Question the Darkness
  Into the Darkness
  Fight the Darkness
  Alone the Darkness
  Lost the Darkness

SEQUEL –
  Matter of Time

Time Piece
Second Chance
Glitch in Time
Our Time
Precious Time

Hidden Secrets Saga:
Download Seventh Mark part 1 For FREE

BOOK TRAILER:

http://www.youtube.com/watch?v=Y-_vVYC1gvo

Like most teenagers, Rouge is trying to figure out who she is and what she wants to be. With little knowledge about her past, she has questions but has never tried to find the answers. Everything changes when she befriends a strangely intoxicating family. Siblings Grace and Michael, appear to have secrets which seem connected to Rouge. Her hunch is confirmed when a horrible incident occurs at an outdoor party. Rouge may be the only one who can find the answer.

An ancient journal, a Sioghra necklace and a special mark force life-altering decisions for a girl who grew up unprepared to fight for her life or others.

All secrets have a cost and Rouge's determination to find the truth can only lead to trouble...or something even more sinister.

RADIUM HALOS - THE SENSELESS SERIES
Book 1 is FREE

Everyone needs to be a hero at one point in their life.

The small town of Elliot Lake will never be the same again.

Caught in a sudden thunderstorm, Zoe, a high school senior from Elliot Lake, and five of her friends take shelter in an abandoned uranium mine. Over the next few days, Zoe's hearing sharpens drastically, beyond what any normal human being can detect. She tells her friends, only to learn that four others have an increased sense as well. Only Kieran, the new boy from Scotland, isn't affected.

Fashioning themselves into superheroes, the group tries to stop the strange occurrences happening in their little town. Muggings, break-ins, disappearances, and murder begin to hit too close to home. It leads the team to think someone knows about their secret - someone who wants them all dead.

An incredulous group of heroes. A traitor in the midst. Some dreams are written in blood.

Courage Runs Red
The Blood Red Series
Book 1 is FREE

WHAT IF COURAGE WAS your only option?

When Kallie lands a college interview with the city's new hot-shot police officer, she has no idea everything in her life is about to change. The detective is young, handsome and seems to have an unnatural ability to stop the increasing local crime rate. Detective Liam's particular interest in Kallie sends her heart and head stumbling over each other.

When a raging blood feud between vampires spills into her home, Kallie gets caught in the middle. Torn between love and family loyalty she must find the courage to fight what she fears the most and possibly risk everything, even if it means dying for those she loves.

Daughter of Darkness
Victoria
Only Death Could Stop Her Now
The Daughters of Darkness is a series of female heroines who may or may not know each other, but all have the same father, Vlad Montour.
Victoria is a Hunter Vampire

Don't miss out!

Click the button below and you can sign up to receive emails whenever W.J. May publishes a new book. There's no charge and no obligation.

https://books2read.com/r/B-A-SSF-LGTR

BOOKS 2 READ

Connecting independent readers to independent writers.

Did you love *Forever*? Then you should read *The Chronicles of Kerrigan Prequel Series Books #1-3* by W.J. May!

A Boxset collection of the first 3 books in the Chronicles of Kerrigan Prequel Series! Fall in love with USA TODAY Bestselling author, W.J. May's international bestselling series. Learn how it all began... before the magic of tatùs.

Christmas Before the Magic - Book #1

When Argyle invites his best friend, Simon Kerrigan, home for the Christmas holidays, he wants to save Simon from staying at Guilder Boarding School on his own.

Simon comes along and doesn't expect to find much more excitement in the tiny Scottish town where Argyle's family lives. Until he meets Beth, Argyle's older sister. She's beautiful, brash and clearly interested in him. When her father warns him to stay away from her, Simon tries, but sometimes destiny has a hope of it's own.

Question the Darkness – Book #2

Learn how it all began ... before Rae Kerrigan.

The sins of the father are the sins of the son.

What did Rae's father do that put fear in people's eyes at the name Kerrigan?

Simon Kerrigan is a bright kid. He likes to ask questions and push adults in their way of thinking. He's falling for a girl he's been warned to stay away from. Tempted by forbidden love, he also must face the biggest challenge of his life: receive a tattoo on his sixteenth birthday.

This ink is going to give him a supernatural ability unlike anyone before him. When secrets of the past begin to reveal themselves, he questions everything he's ever known.

Pressure from Guilder Boarding School and the Privy Council only confuse Simon more as he struggles to find himself.

How hard will he have to shake the family tree to find the truth about the past?

The Chronicles of Kerrigan Prequel is the beginning of the story before Rae Kerrigan. Christmas Before the Magic is just the beginning (but not the end...)

Into the Darkness – Book #3

What did Rae's father do that put fear in people's eyes at the name Kerrigan?

After a mysterious attempt is made on his life, Simon Kerrigan has more questions than ever, and this time, he's not the only one. The beginnings of a secret society are formed at Guilder. A society of other like-minded students all unsatisfied with the status quo. All searching for the truth.

But things aren't always as they seem.

When Simon gets an unexpected visitor, his entire world is turned up-side-down. Suddenly, the rules that were made to keep him safe, are the only things standing in his way.

Who can he trust? Can he learn to master his tatù? Most importantly, can he do it in time to protect those things that are most precious to him?

Prequel Series:

Christmas Before the Magic

Question the Darkness

Into the Darkness

Fight the Darkness

Alone in the Darkness

Lost in Darkness

The Chronicles of Kerrigan Series

Rae of Hope

Dark Nebula

House of Cards

Royal Tea

Under Fire

End in Sight

Hidden Darkness

Twisted Together

Mark of Fate

Strength & Power

Last One Standing

Rae of Light

The Chronicles of Kerrigan Sequel

A Matter of Time

Time Piece

Second Chance

Glitch in Time
Our Time
Precious Time
    The Chronicles of Kerrigan: Gabriel
Living in the Past
Present for Today
Staring at the Future

Also by W.J. May

Bit-Lit Series
Lost Vampire
Cost of Blood
Price of Death

Blood Red Series
Courage Runs Red
The Night Watch
Marked by Courage
Forever Night

Daughters of Darkness: Victoria's Journey
Victoria
Huntress
Coveted (A Vampire & Paranormal Romance)
Twisted

Hidden Secrets Saga

Seventh Mark - Part 1
Seventh Mark - Part 2
Marked By Destiny
Compelled
Fate's Intervention
Chosen Three
The Hidden Secrets Saga: The Complete Series

Paranormal Huntress Series
Never Look Back
Coven Master
Alpha's Permission

Prophecy Series
Only the Beginning
White Winter
Secrets of Destiny

The Chronicles of Kerrigan
Rae of Hope
Dark Nebula
House of Cards
Royal Tea
Under Fire
End in Sight
Hidden Darkness
Twisted Together
Mark of Fate

Strength & Power
Last One Standing
Rae of Light
The Chronicles of Kerrigan Box Set Books # 1 - 6

The Chronicles of Kerrigan: Gabriel
Living in the Past
Staring at the Future
Present For Today

The Chronicles of Kerrigan Prequel
Question the Darkness
Into the Darkness
Fight the Darkness
Alone in the Darkness
Lost in Darkness
Christmas Before the Magic
The Chronicles of Kerrigan Prequel Series Books #1-3

The Chronicles of Kerrigan Sequel
A Matter of Time
Time Piece
Second Chance
Glitch in Time
Our Time
Precious Time

The Hidden Secrets Saga
Seventh Mark (part 1 & 2)

The Queen's Alpha Series
Eternal
Everlasting
Unceasing
Evermore
Forever
Boundless

The Senseless Series
Radium Halos
Radium Halos - Part 2
Nonsense

Standalone
Shadow of Doubt (Part 1 & 2)
Five Shades of Fantasy
Shadow of Doubt - Part 1
Shadow of Doubt - Part 2
Four and a Half Shades of Fantasy
Dream Fighter
What Creeps in the Night
Forest of the Forbidden
Arcane Forest: A Fantasy Anthology

Made in the USA
Monee, IL
22 October 2020

45787467R00115